Reeya's Earth Day

Reeya's Earth Day

A Social Justice Primer for the 98%

by

Dan Camilli

Seven
Iron
Press

Copyright © 2019 Dan Camilli

ISBN 978-1-0912038-6-0
Seven Iron Press

Cover and interior design by Colby Groves

For Reeya, and her generation.

May they have the wisdom, compassion and courage to stride towards Social, Economic and Environmental Justice.

Preface

This book was literally more than three decades in the making.

For many years, my students urged me to record my classroom presentations and post them on YouTube or some other Millennial-friendly cyberspace hang out. And for just as long, I have politely declined to do so.

My resistance to record classes stems from my deep- seated belief that an authentic learning environment must be free of any inhibitions to wide-ranging exploration and discovery. I believe that the classroom environment is a very Zen-like experience; that no two classes are ever the same and that recording devices of any kind serve to stifle the candid engagement in what I refer to as an Authentic Learning Experience (AKA: <u>The Now!</u>).

Authentic learning can only occur as part of an organic process that imposes minimal strictures on student and teacher as they examine an event or historical figure ("Thinking Allowed"). I am such a firm believer in this made-from-scratch methodology that I refrain from the now common practice of power point presentations, viewing them as too pre-fabricated and instead, employ only whiteboard and marker to jot down key concepts and ideas for our collective consideration.

Indeed, I am such an adamant devotee of this organic approach that I will usually erase the previous classes' notes and start entirely anew with the next class. While this may present more work for me, I believe that I owe the Authentic Learning Experience to every student and that requires that we collectively draw up our own, organic points of discourse, employing my notes only as a general guideline.

This is not to suggest that I have never been tempted to record a class experience, especially after walking out of a particularly electrifying lecture/discussion buzzing from the dynamic energy we had collectively generated around a topic of intense interest to us all- whether it be the dark legacy of slavery and institutional racism or the establishment of the American Ruling Class in the form of the Robber Barons or the on-going struggle of workers to organize and, attain their fair share of the profits that they themselves create.

Perhaps wisdom comes with age. I can only hope so, as I have most recently and reluctantly arrived at the conclusion that my students may have a point. I now feel some sense of urgency in needing to record, in some fashion, the essential teachings of our collective class experiences. That is the purpose of this book.

After decades spent teaching history and philosophy classes and being honored with student and peer awards- including the Fulbright Distinguished Awards in Teaching Scholarship, Keizai Koho Fellowship, Massachusetts Teacher of the Year Nomination and, one of my most prized possessions, boxes filled with cards, handwritten by students (and parents) expressing their appreciation for the ways in which our class experience had transformed the way they see the world, I now wished to provide readers with something resembling, however inadequately, the dynamic, transformative power of our collective classroom experience.

The essential elements of many of my core lectures are presented here by veteran teacher and long-time social activist Mike Antonelli as well as a fictional account of the transformational power of the experience upon one student, Reeya Patel. This is then, not so much a work of fiction as a fictional account of facts.

This is the coming-of-age story of high school senior, Reeya Patel, who has her social conscience and consciousness awakened by Earth Day Keynote Speaker, Mike Antonelli's presentation and, consequently commits herself to becoming an activist, a change agent for justice. Using the student presentation topics of Labor, Education and Earth Day as a point of entry, Antonelli employs history, sociology, psychology, political science and economics in describing the long, hard struggle of working class people of every ethnic background, race and gender to attain economic, social, political and environmental justice. He provides the class and the reader with an outline summary of how we now find ourselves in this present political landscape and, along the way, defines critical terms and concepts such as The Right, The Left, the Dominant Narrative, and Asymmetric Polarization. He also describes the economic policies of the Republicans and Democrats while also dispelling unwarranted fears of Democratic Socialism- an approach he says, that's as American as apple pie or Franklin D. Roosevelt and Lyndon Baines Johnson. Antonelli explains that Democratic Socialism is simply a governmental manifestation of what he refers to as **"Radical Empathy."**

Antonelli's presentation becomes a deeply transformational experience for Reeya, who finally sees the vital importance of political engagement and commits herself to becoming an active change agent in what she now understands is a power relationship between the working and ruling class.

By faithfully presenting some core teachings of my classes, through the voice of Mike Antonelli and Ms. Randi Kaufman's

Social Studies class at Cesar Chavez High School, I hope to provide the reader with a primer for action on behalf of social justice that presents them with some powerful analytical tools, guides them along the confluence of historical events, demonstrates the ways by which one connects the dots of history seeking patterns and themes in order to better understand the power relationships that oppress all working people regardless of ethnicity, race, gender or sexual orientation.

From time to time you may notice some repetition. This is attributable to either poor editing or good pedagogy as I will at times, repeat an important concept and perhaps link it to some other significant event or idea. To this end, repetition is not necessarily redundancy. There is, indeed, some method behind the madness.

This book is then, a primer for social consciousness, conscience and civic action. A Social Justice Primer for the 98% that comprises the working class. As a Primer, it is deliberately designed as an overview, a macro, big- picture perspective of the present political landscape and some of the major historical events that brought us to where we are today. It is presented as an outline; a guide to further study by the reader. Designed not as an academic work but rather a working person's guide to public policy, it is intentionally unencumbered by excessive footnotes and citations.

One of my inspirations for writing this book was the huge impact that Classic Comics and Classics Illustrated comic books had upon me as a kid. Indeed, Classic Comics and Classics Illustrated were often my introduction to the literary canon which included titles like Moby Dick, Robin Hood, Robinson Crusoe and Treasure Island. I have many fond memories of leaving dusty old Mac's Smoke Shop with a paper bag containing a 15 cent Classic Comic, a nickel Hershey Bar and ten cent bottle of Coca Cola, heading home for an afternoon of what I then considered Paradise. These inexpensive, accessible and user-friendly comic book narratives inspired me to further explore the world of ideas, just as I hope that this modest primer will further motivate readers to explore the world of government, public policy and social justice. Every effort is made to present concepts in the most simple, straightforward terms possible, adhering to Einstein's observation that ***"You do not really understand something unless you can explain it to your grandmother."*** So this one's for you, Nonna! Che tu possa riposare in pace.

The book, like my lectures, is liberally peppered with quotes from prominent thinkers which appear in ***bold italicized*** print. I have done so in order to encourage further investigation by the reader. In contrast, my own key concepts and essential ideas derived from dog-eared lecture notes, are in **standard bold** type. Readers are encouraged to pursue further study with the assistance of the "Books to Hang Out With" section located in the back of the book, just before the blank page provided for your notes.

I hope that you enjoy Reeya's Earth Day, but more importantly, I hope that, you, like Reeya, will be inspired to become more actively engaged in the struggle for economic, social, political, and environmental justice. To that end, this book is intended as an introduction and not the final word on any topic. It should be considered a first and not final step upon your path to becoming a more informed and active change agent on behalf of a more humane, sustainable culture and planet.   In solidarity.

Sincerely,

Dan Camilli

Austin, Texas
Spring, 2019

Table of Contents

Introduction

"May you live in interesting times."

(Anonymous–Origins unknown. Considered by some to be an
ancient Chinese curse.)

The Chinese often define "interesting" as difficult, troubling,
and challenging. By that measure, we do, alas, live in very
"interesting" times. The nation is more socio-politically divided
than at any time since the Civil War

This book is a response to the "interesting" times in which we
live. It is, as the title states, a Primer. It is designed to be a short,
informative introduction which will hopefully, inspire the reader
to further study and social engagement. In addition to providing
a short list of "Books to Hang Out With," I have deliberately
quoted thinkers from a wide variety of backgrounds and beliefs
and encourage you to look them up and learn more about them.
Their names and quotes are in **_bold italics_** while my key concepts are printed in **bold type**. (Without Italics)

Reeya's transformation from apathetic high school senior to av-
idly committed activist is a social conscience coming-of-age sto-

ry for our "interesting" time. Her inspirational awakening and commitment to the practice of Radical Empathy/Democratic Socialism on behalf of the struggling 98% is a sorely needed life-affirming example for us all. If her story provides but one reader with a sense of commitment to the practice of radical empathy and activism on behalf of social justice, it will have been well worth telling.

Chapter 1

The Big Day Arrives!

"Wake up, Reeya!" Mrs. Patel shouted up the stairs toward her daughter's bedroom, "You'll be late for school."

"I'm up! I'm up! No need to worry, mother," replied Reeya, "I wouldn't miss the big Earth Day celebration we've all been planning the whole school year! I wouldn't miss it for the world," chuckled Reeya, enjoying her own word play.

Reeya scrambled out of bed, and quickly showered, dressed and carefully collected all materials for her presentation on the origins and history of Earth Day.

Earth Day was, without a doubt, the single biggest event of the year in Ms. Randi Kaufman's Social Studies class at Cesar Chavez High School and the main reason that so many students flock each year to register for her courses. The Earth Day Celebration was the culminating event in the most popular class taught by the most popular teacher on campus.

The morning of the big day was devoted to student presentations on issues impacting the earth and its wellbeing including, of course, issues of social, political, economic as well as environmental justice. Student presentations were followed by a potluck luncheon and a special cake, featuring the Earth Day flag, baked in honor of the occasion. The afternoon was reserved for the keynote address by a speaker selected by Ms. Kaufman and her students to cap off the Earth Day festivities.

This year's guest speaker is educator, community organizer and social activist Mike Antonelli, a teacher who has been involved in social justice activism since the Viet Nam War and civil rights struggles of the 1960's.

Students eagerly clamored into Ms. Kaufman's room as the day's opening bell rang out through the halls, lugging their power point USB flash drives, charts, graphs, models and binders, all carefully prepared for their presentations.

"Did you remember everything?" asked Reeya's project partner, Fiorella Reyes. Together, they had spent countless afternoons in the library and long evenings at each other's homes working on their presentation as their parents fed them adhirasam (an Indian rice flour cookie) and mazapanes (a traditional Mexican sweet treat). And today was the day they would present the fruit of their labor; a presentation on the origins and history of Earth Day itself! The two young ladies could barely contain their excitement but knew that they would have to wait their turn while enjoying other group presentations. Ms. Kaufman had posted the presentation schedule on the class bulletin board and, fittingly, the Earth Day presentation would be the very last of the morning.

"Good morning, and happy Earth Day, class!" began Ms. K., with a notable hint of excitement in her voice, as students settled into their desks with their project partners and presentation materials. "Welcome to our annual Earth Day Celebration! We have a wonderful day of festivities before us beginning with student group presentations this morning. Our honored guest today is Mr. Mike Antonelli, longtime teacher and social justice activist, who will speak to us at the conclusion of the day's events and will assist me in judging and commenting on student presentations this morning."

Chapter 2

First Student Presentation: Plight of the Working Class

"Our first presentation topic is 'The Plight of the Working Class: from The Gilded Age to Today' by Erin Kelly and Jamal Williams." announced Ms. Kaufman, "You have the floor." as she sank into a student desk next to Guest Speaker, Mike Antonelli.

Erin and Jamal quickly pinned up their posters and charts as Jamal nervously addressed the class. "Good Morning. Our presentation begins during America's Gilded Age 1870-1890. During the period after the Civil War, when American industry moved swiftly into mechanization and mass production. This was a period of great inventions and innovations that were, sadly, mostly enjoyed by a small portion of the general population as the poor and working classes were subjected to low wages, dangerous working conditions, and long hours in order to enrich the so-called 'Captains of Industry' also known as 'Robber Barons' such as Andrew Carnegie, John D. Rockefeller and J.P. Morgan.

"In fact, the term 'Gilded Age' was coined by American writer and satirist Mark Twain who likened the period to a piece of gilded jewelry which looks lovely until you scratch beneath the surface and see the ugly cheap metal within. He astutely observed that this was indeed a period of great inventions and innovations–the lightbulb, telephone and even skyscrapers were products of this period–but at what cost? And that's what Erin and I researched. Our essential questions were: *What was the human and environmental cost of this rapid industrialization process and who benefitted? Have conditions improved for the working class since then? And does the capitalist class still reap most of the benefits of workers labor today?*

"With the introduction of mass production, and especially after the conclusion of the Civil War, the new factories were desperate for workers." continued Jamal. "This was, unsurprisingly, the period in which America welcomed new immigrants fleeing oppression, famine, poverty and persecution in places such as Ireland, Italy, Poland, and Russia. These groups collectively are referred to as 'New Immigrants' and they were very different from the 'Old Immigrants.' Unlike the Old Immigrants who hailed from northern and western Europe and consisted of the English, Germans and Scandinavians, the New Immigrants, arrived mostly after 1880, and were from southern and eastern Europe. They often did not speak English; were darker skinned and of a different religion than the White Anglo Saxon Protestants that made up the majority of Old Immigrants.

"The Old Immigrants–which included most of the Robber Barons–could not live with nor without the New Immigrants. Many disliked their cultures, languages and looks and viewed them as an 'anti-American' threat and even as sub-humans, but desperately needed them to work in the factories and endure the soul-killing drudgery of assembly lines at subsistence wages for long hours each day–six days per week. In short, the newly established industries, located largely in the North which had, ironically, fought a war to eliminate slavery were now creating a new form of servitude called wage slavery.

"The human and environmental cost of the Gilded Age is immense," continued Jamal, "when one considers the millions of men, women and children condemned to a life of poverty and hand-to-mouth subsistence and the unrestricted pollution of the land, waters and air. Living in rat infested cold water flats and tenement apartments, these people worked twelve or more hours per day, six days per week, in workplaces rife with hazardous conditions. This workforce included children who were not even teenagers, mining coal, and working on assembly lines.

"The dehumanization of the assembly line worker was essentially perfected with the introduction of so-called 'Scientific Management' by a man named **Frederick Winslow Taylor (1856-1915),** considered one of the first management consultants and a leader of the **'Efficiency Movement.'** While widely commended by the wealthy and managerial classes, perhaps no one has done more to degrade and dehumanize the worker than Taylor, who, in 1911, published his 'efficiency techniques' in ***The Principles of Scientific Management***. The principles presented in his book became widely known as **'Taylorism'** and have long been the bane of working class existence from New Immigrant workers sweatshops to today's multinational corporate manufacturing plants."

"Taylor was a mechanical engineer by training and viewed the typical factory workplace as riddled with inefficiencies." said Erin, taking over the narrative. "These 'inefficiencies' included what would be considered normal human interaction and movement on the assembly line, which he worked to restrict. Workers were literally instructed as to the correct way to turn their bodies when working the assembly line in order to minimize 'wasted' motions and time. The purpose and result was to further fragmentize tasks and better control workers thus maximizing production and profits.

"Taylor would break down a task into its most simple, elemental pieces and strive to eliminate any non-essential skills from the labor process—making shop floor workers interchangeable and expendable while undermining craft unions. **Taylor believed that the most severe divisions of labor best served both productivity and social control.** All manual work was to be reduced to a standardized rubric and his time and motion studies insured the maximum production from every worker on the assembly line.

"Taylor went even further," Erin said, "by separating mental work from manual labor. He vested management with all matters conceptual and relegated the manual labor to the shop floor workers, who were to serve as 'human tools' of management—their only responsibility was to mindlessly follow directions and consistently repeat their limited and motion—restricted tasks; perhaps, putting the same nut on the same bolt for hours on end. Thinking and conceptualizing about the work was for those 'above their pay scale' in management who wore ties and white collars in sharp contrast to the workmen's blue collar. **Taylorism served not only to further widen the worker-management divide but advanced the notion of a professional managerial class which would serve as enforcers on behalf of the wealthy- keeping the workers in line and on task.**

"Controlling worker's physical movements, reducing their work to the most elementary tasks while removing their participation in the conceptualization process greatly increased the stress, dissociation and general misery of many millions condemned to life in the working classes."

At this point, Mr. Antonelli interjected with a question. "Why, exactly, is this period and the plight of these people relevant today?"

Jamal considered the question for a moment then replied, **"Wage slavery still exists today. It can be found throughout the**

fast food industry, in retailing and other service industries as well as manufacturing. Much of the manufacturing work has now been outsourced overseas to places like China, Mexico, Guatemala and the like, where wages and working conditions are even worse than in the U.S.. Corporations, some of the same ones that existed during the Gilded Age, have relocated their manufacturing operations to these countries seeking to exploit even more vulnerable people with even less interference from unions, taxes and government regulation. As industries' wealth and power grew, multi-national corporations spanned out across the globe seeking the lowest wage workers. Today, it's a race to the bottom for most working people across the planet." concluded Jamal.

"Excellent answer!" exclaimed Ms. Kaufman, nodding her head in agreement with Mr. Antonelli.

Continuing, Jamal said, "The plight of immigrants today in the U.S. is not unlike that of the Gilded Age. They are largely viewed with suspicion, and work long hours at low wage jobs. The faces change but the game remains the same; to exploit the labor of newcomers and the powerless."

"Then why do they continue to come to a country where they will be treated in such a dehumanizing way?" asked, Ms. Kaufman.

"I got this, Jamal." said Erin placing her hand on his elbow. "Most people do not willingly choose to leave their own culture to live in another with unfamiliar customs and language but are driven by economic necessity to do so. They do, in fact, come in search of a better life for themselves and their children. Unfortunately what all too many discover is that the same economic system that oppressed them in their native land continues to exploit them here, perhaps a tad less severely, but, sadly, it's only a matter of degree.

"Immigrants also provide a pretty accurate barometer on the state of our economy." continued Erin. "Indeed, American attitudes towards immigrants provides a fairly accurate snapshot of the economy at any given time. When things are good, immigrants are often welcomed and viewed as hard working people striving for a better life. But when the economy takes a downward turn, they are seen as foreigners stealing precious jobs away from hard working American citizens. They are also then often unjustly viewed as a criminal element and lazy scofflaws taking advantage of welfare, food stamps and other social programs, even though they actually don't qualify to receive most public assistance and statistically commit fewer crimes than American born citizens."

"Very well put," interrupted Antonelli. "I'll actually have more to say about that economic system in my talk this afternoon," he said with a knowing smile.

Erin then continued, "So the exploitation of labor which gained a firm foothold in the United States after the so-called abolition of slavery is very much still with us today. But today wage slavery poses a global threat to the quality of life for the majority of the planet's inhabitants. Ironically, Frederick Winslow Taylor's mother, Emily, was an Abolitionist. Apparently her compassionate concern for the plight of bondage slaves did not transfer to her son, who exhibited callous disregard for the wage slaves whose lives he made so much more miserable in the name of 'efficiency.'"

Meanwhile, Reeya, who had been listening carefully to what was being said while trying to keep from thinking about her own pending presentation, thoughtfully raised her hand and said, "The conditions you describe are very much present today in my parent's native land of India but what can we do about this?"

Erin responded, "Well, first off, everyone must use their power as consumers to reject products produced through wage slavery. We must educate people to use the power of their purses to say no to the exploitation of workers anywhere on the planet. And help all consumers to understand that while lower prices may be tempting, the real human cost of that purchase is the continued enslavement of other people who also have hopes, dreams and families just like ourselves. We must support the organization of labor unions worldwide and elect public officials who insist on labor rights when negotiating international trade deals and treaties."

"An American author named **Upton Sinclair**", Jamal added, "had a major impact on the regulation of the meat packing industry when, in 1906, he wrote ***The Jungle***. A fictional account of the true-to-life working conditions in Chicago's meat packing industry. Sinclair provided graphic descriptions of both the brutal working and living conditions of the assembly line workers as well as the horrific lack of sanitation standards in meat preparation. Sinclair's intent was to expose the inhuman conditions and subsistence wages suffered by workers but, tellingly, the public was mostly focused on food purity and pressured the government to pass the Pure Food and Drug Act and Meat Inspection Act, considered to be the first federal laws regulating an industry. As Mr. Sinclair put it, *'I aimed at the public's heart, and by accident I hit it in the stomach.'*

"None the less", continued Jamal, "Sinclair's book demonstrated the ability to raise public awareness and mobilize people to demand change."

"As well as the importance of free speech and a free press." added Erin.

"Any other questions for Erin and Jamal?" asked Ms. Kaufman, surveying the room for any raised hands.

Seeing none, she said, "Thank you both for an informative and thought-provoking presentation."

The two then took their seats to a round of polite applause.

"Mr. Antonelli, would you be so kind as to introduce our second presentation team?" asked Ms. Kaufman, passing him an index card.

"Why, I'd be honored to do so, Ms. Kaufman", said a smiling Antonelli. "Our next presentation," he announced, reading Ms. K's note card, "is 'Public Education and Its Role in American Society' by Nikki Sterns and Tony Donatello."

Chapter 3

Second Student Presentation: Public Education

Nikki began pinning up charts on the board as Tony addressed the class. "Good morning everyone," he said nervously. "Nikki and I have chosen the topic of public education for our presentation. We discovered, much to our surprise, that our public schools have long been threatened by all sorts of special interests and are presently in a state of rapid transformation due to a number of factors including the global economy, and new technology. But first we'll present a brief overview of the origins of public schools and their proposed purposes.

"The first public schools in the thirteen American colonies", continued Tony, "were established in Boston in 1635. The Boston Latin School, then funded by donations and land rentals, is the first public school and the oldest existing, operating school in the United States. The first free taxpayer supported school in North America, The Mather School, opened its doors in Dorchester, Massachusetts in 1639. Because their religious beliefs stressed the importance of reading the Bible, Puritans of the Massachusetts colony passed the 'Olde Deluder Satan' Act of 1647 which required that any town with more than 50 households appoint a town teacher and towns with more than 100 households were required to establish an elementary school in order to insure that children were literate and thus able to read the scriptures which they believed served to save them from that 'Olde Deluder Satan.'

"Due in large part to slavery," continued Tony, "the southern colonies found themselves well behind New England in the creation of public schools since the planter class resisted public schools-viewing the education of indentured servants and later African slaves as a threat to their privileged status in the social order. The wealthy planters would, instead, hire private tutors or send their sons to private academies. It would not be until after the Civil War, that newly elected Republican governments would establish tax supported public schools in the south. These schools would admit both whites and blacks but it was generally agreed that the public schools would be racially segregated. The few integrated public schools in the south were located in New Orleans. Unsurprisingly, public schools for blacks were consistently underfunded until the landmark Supreme Court decision of Brown v. Board of Education in 1954, which declared that the establishment of separate schools for whites and blacks was unconstitutional." concluded Tony.

"Nikki, you want to take it from here?" asked Tony.

"Sure, I got this." she confidently said. "I'm going to discuss the history of education for women and girls" she began. "The Catholic Ursaline Academy in New Orleans has the distinction of being the oldest continually operating school for girls in the United States. The Sisters of Saint Ursula established the Academy in 1727 and it was the first free school to teach both free and enslaved women of color as well as Native American women. It was also Louisiana's first school of music and first boarding school for girls. The earliest tax supported schools for girls can be traced to

New England as far back as 1767. However, not all towns complied with the tax and the availability of female public education was largely dependent on your location.

"Public education expanded greatly during the Progressive Era (1890's -1930's) as America's cities teemed with fast growing new immigrant populations from southern and eastern Europe as well as China and elsewhere. A product largely of the urban ruling elite, public schools rapidly developed very regimented curricula designed to achieve the goal of assimilation in order to assuage the fears of Old Immigrants that these newcomers might challenge their power and influence by bringing what they considered 'un-American' beliefs, values and behaviors to the United States.

"This assimilation process," said Nikki, "explains why so few second and third generation children of New Immigrants spoke the language of their hereditary motherlands. The focus was on discipline, obedience and patriotism. Indeed, it was during this time that American flags were prominently displayed in every classroom and later, daily recitation of the Pledge of Allegiance became common practices in America's public schools."

"In many ways, public schools have been ground zero for the playing out of often conflicting goals and values in American life", continued Tony. "The schools have provided the stage for national debates over racial segregation, income inequality, vocational training and religious teachings to name but a few.

"Today, public schools, which still educate the vast majority of our increasingly multiracial population, find themselves in the crosshairs of a decades-long attempt to undermine and discredit their important work and mission. Public schools are being undermined by several factions with often conflicting interests and goals including private sector for-profit companies that falsely claim that they can produce better results and outcomes than our professionally trained and certified public school teachers. They have often used their formidable financial resources to denigrate public schools and public school teachers, falsely claiming that their standardized testing to cookbook curriculum approach will produce better results even though the preponderance of evidence demonstrates otherwise.

"Sadly, they have managed to purchase a sizable media presence which has served to convince much of the public of their largely false claims. The introduction of privately operated Charter Schools has served to siphon away badly needed financial resources from public school systems which were already reeling from years of Draconian budget cuts. Their objectives," Tony said, "like any business, are first and always to profit from our children's education and even more concerning, control the curriculum that children experience, eliminating the critical and creative thinking process attained through more traditional Socratic style learning, exploration and discovery. This 'drill and kill', teach-to-the-test approach serves to produce more docile, less engaged citizens and employees. This all serves to better control the masses on behalf of the wealthy who, of course, would never subject their own children to such a mind- numbing experience disguised as education."

"This approach," added Nikki, "is a logical extension of what was originally considered a not so subtle primary purpose of public education-namely, to assimilate the young and teach them to accept the social and economic injustice put upon them by the wealthy classes. It is nothing short of a hostile corporate takeover of public education designed to extract profit for the capitalists while producing a generation of submissive, subservient cubicle farm animals to serve the objectives of their rich corporate masters. Multiple studies determine that Charter Schools, be they so-called public or private, do no better and indeed often worse with regards to meeting measured learning outcomes and standardized tests than do public schools.

"This is, arguably, the single most important struggle taking place today," Nikki concluded, "since the very consciousness and conscience of the next generation of working class Americans lies in the balance. And that concludes our presentation on Public Education."

"Any questions?" asked Ms. Kaufman. Seeing no raised hands, she thanked Nikki and Tony for their presentation and they made their way back to their seats accompanied by approving applause from their classmates.

Chapter 4

Reeya's and Fiorella's Earth Day Presentation

"Finally! it's our turn to present," thought Reeya as Ms. K. beckoned her and Fiorella to the front of the class.

Reeya, now a bit more nervous than she thought she'd be, warily said, "Good morning, everyone. Fiorella and I decided to do our project on Earth Day itself. We call our presentation 'The Origins of Earth Day and Its Importance Today.'

"When we first went to the library to begin researching the history of Earth Day, the librarian, Ms. Harney, smiled and asked us which Earth Day we were researching. Puzzled, we asked her 'What do you mean?' She informed us that there are in fact two distinct Earth Days. The first is the **Equinox Earth Day**. This one is celebrated annually world-wide on the Vernal Equinox, which is always either March 20th or 21st. Then there's what's simply called **Earth Day**, which is celebrated each year on April 22. So, for the sake of clarity I will refer to the two Earth Days as the Equinox Earth Day, celebrated on the Vernal Equinox and the other, we will refer to as April Earth Day, celebrated on April 22nd.

"It's important to note that both Earth Days have had a major impact globally." continued Reeya. "Both Earth Days were products of the rapidly changing cultural values brought about as a result of major events of the 1960's. Earth Day was the result of what historians call a **Zeitgeist,** a German word which loosely translates as 'the spirit of the times'. The 1960's were a period of tremendous social and cultural upheaval as young people, who came to be called Baby Boomers, challenged established cultural practices and questioned authority in all aspects of life including protests in support of Civil Rights and in opposition to the Viet Nam War.

"There were also major events which raised public awareness of environmental issues," added Reeya, "including, in 1962, the publication of *Silent Spring* by **Rachel Carson (1907-1964)**, a marine biologist and conservationist, who described the role of synthetic pesticides in the destruction of the environment. Carson also detailed the efforts of chemical corporations to intentionally engage in a disinformation campaign, designed to convince the public that these pesticides, such as DDT, were safe to use. And perhaps worse yet, Rachel Carson's book included reports of government officials accepting chemical industry claims without scientific verification. Needless to say, Ms. Carson's book was met with powerful opposition from the chemical industry but it did lead to a nation-wide ban on the use of DDT and inspired the rise of the environmental movement. In 1980, in recognition of this women's courage and perseverance in defense of our planet, Rachel Carson was posthumously awarded the Presidential Medal of Freedom, the highest award given by the United States by President Jimmy Carter."

Reeya continued, "The citation on Ms. Carson's medal reads: **Rachel Carson** 'Never silent, herself, in the face of destructive trends, Rachel Carson fed a spring of awareness across America and beyond. A biologist with a gentle, clear voice, she welcomed her audiences to her love of the sea, while with an equally clear determined voice she warned Americans of the dangers human beings themselves pose for their own environment. Always concerned, always eloquent, she created a tide of environmental consciousness that has not ebbed.'"

Fiorella then said, "Another major event which led to the creation of both Earth Days occurred towards the conclusion of this tumultuous and transformative decade, in 1969. In January and February of that year an offshore oil well blowout spilled between 80 and 100 thousand barrels of crude oil onto the beautiful beaches of Santa Barbara County, California, killing tens of thousands of seabirds, fish, seals, sea lions and dolphins. It was the biggest oil spill on record in US waters at the time and is still the biggest ever off the California coast. Reports of the spill and photographs and video coverage of the environmental carnage stirred outrage in the American public which set the stage for the creation of Earth Day.

"The Equinox Earth Day, first celebrated on March 21, 1970, was the creation of newspaper publisher and social activist **John McConnell (1915-2012)**. It is celebrated annually on the vernal equinox, either March 20 or 21st because this is when day and night are exactly the same length everywhere on the planet, symbolizing the balance and symmetry of nature. Being the first day of spring in the Northern hemisphere and of autumn in the southern hemisphere, it is, appropriately, a day of change and renewal. By the way, the spring equinox in the southern hemisphere on September 21 is also celebrated as the International Day of Peace.

"San Francisco Mayor, Joseph Alioto signed the first Earth Day Proclamation on March 21, 1970, after Mr. McConnell had introduced the idea for a planetary Earth Day celebration at the 1969 UNESCO Conference on the Environment.

"Mr. McConnell explained that the purpose of Earth Day was to remind all people of our shared responsibility to protect, honor and celebrate our planet," continued Fiorella. "John McConnell's dream of an international day to honor the planet was more fully realized when on February 26, 1971, then United Nations General Secretary U Thant signed a proclamation declaring that the U.N. would celebrate Earth Day on the occasion of the Vernal Equinox by ringing the Peace Bell (a gift from Japan) at its New York Headquarters. Today, the ringing of bells simultaneously with the UN Peace Bell, in commemoration and celebration of Earth Day, is a very common practice worldwide.

"'Earth Day is natures' day.' said Mr. McConnell in a 1991 Celebrate Earth Day speech at the United Nations, *'A day of drama, dreams and dedication to the restoration, renewal, and improvement of Earth's natural beauty and bounty.'*

"McConnell, believing that Earth Day needed a powerful symbol representing what he saw as a new, emerging global consciousness, created the Earth Flag. Originally, the now iconic banner featured a two color silk screened depiction of the earth deliberately omitting any individual countries which might suggest boundaries or borders. This was later replaced by a color photo of Earth, depicting the 'big blue marble' we call home taken from space by NASA astronauts. The flag perfectly represented McConnell's *'Unity in Diversity'* principle as it vividly depicted the beauty and fragility of our home planet. Over the years, many luminaries from diverse walks of life have expressed their support for Earth Day and its values. In 1978, world renowned anthropologist **Margaret Mead (1901-1978)** expressed her support for the Equinox Earth Day in a statement, which read in part:

'Earth Day is the first holy day which transcends all national borders, yet preserves all geographical integ-

rities, spans mountains and oceans and time belts, and yet brings people all over the world into one resonating accord, is devoted to the preservation of the harmony in nature and yet draws upon the triumphs of technology, the measurement of time, and instantaneous communication through space.'" (Margaret Mead, "Earth Day," EPA Journal, March 1978.)

"Meanwhile, in a kind of parallel universe, another Earth Day was being created," said Reeya, taking over the narrative from Fiorella. "It was first celebrated on April 22, 1970 and is considered to be the idea of Wisconsin Senator Gaylord Nelson, who, after the 1969 Santa Barbara Oil Spill, sought to mobilize the then powerful anti-war/pro civil rights student movement on campuses across the nation on behalf of the environment. In fact, Senator Nelson announced a 'National Teach-In Day on the Environment' (Earth Day) celebration for April 22, 1970 because it fell between Spring Break and Final Exams on most campuses. It was a bipartisan initiative as Democratic Senator Gaylord Nelson was joined by then Republican Pete McCloskey as Co-Chairs of Earth Day. Senator Nelson then asked Harvard's Denis Hayes to become Coordinator of the first April Earth Day celebration. Nelson, McCloskey and Hayes hoped to bring together diverse groups around protecting the planet and advancing conservationism and environmental justice. And the first April Earth Day did just that as thousands of universities, colleges, high schools as well as everyday citizens participated in demonstrations and marched on behalf of the planet.

"The environment would now take its proper place as a major political issue and the environmental movement would see its growing people power lead to the creation of the U.S. Environmental Protection Agency (1970) as well as other landmark legislation such as the Clean Air Act (1970), Clean Water Act (1972) and the Endangered Species Act (1973).

"Nelson described his vision for the movement in his speech at the first April Earth Day celebration in 1970: *'Our goal is an environment of decency, quality, and mutual respect for all other human creatures and for all living creatures. The battle to restore a proper relationship between man, his environment and other living creatures will require a long, sustained, political, moral, ethical and financial commitment—far beyond any effort made before.'* (Source: https://www.thespruce.com/gaylord-nelson-and-earth-day-1708729)

"On April Earth Day's twentieth anniversary, in 1990, the celebration coordinators decided to take the April Earth Day global by celebrating on a worldwide scale, organizing over 200 million people in over 140 countries on behalf of planetary and environmental justice. This would lead to the 1992 United Nations Earth Summit in Rio de Janeiro, Brazil.

"To better insure the future of the April Earth Day celebrations, Senator Nelson and program organizers formed Earth Day USA which not only coordinated the next five April Earth Day celebrations but also created the website **EarthDay.org.** After the 25th Anniversary celebration in 1995, organizing responsibilities were entrusted to the Earth Day Network. The Earth Day Network would now coordinate Earth Day celebrations and also produce educational materials regarding a wide range of environmental issues.

"In 1995, President Bill Clinton awarded Senator Gaylord Nelson the Presidential Medal of Freedom, the nation's highest civilian honor in recognition of his founding of the April Earth Day.

"April Earth Day, 2000," Reeya continued, "marked the first time the event went online–using the internet to bring together over 5,000 environmental groups and hundreds of millions of people in over 180 countries across the planet. Speakers included actor

Leonardo DiCaprio and Vice President Al Gore.

"Today, Earth Day and its numerous supporting organizations continue to organize and coordinate the holiday celebration and provide educational programs and information to individuals and groups on a wide range of environmental issues. Their work has become even more significant with the planet facing the ever more troubling impact of climate change and global warming."

Global Warming and Climate Change

"Whether you're a Climate Change believer or denier," continued Reeya, "there can be no disputing the fact that the planet is warming up. Scientists report that in 2016 the earth reached its highest temperature on record; breaking a record set the year before which broke the record set in the year before that–marking the first time since such records have been kept that temperature records had been broken in three consecutive years! So there can be no doubting that the planet is warming. In fact, the warmest years on record are ten of the last twelve years, according to NASA Surface Data Analysis.

"The question, however, is 'why?'" Reeya asked. "The earth has experienced warming patterns in the past but none as dramatically swift as the present one which indicates that something or someone is causing the temperature to warm and scientists have overwhelmingly concluded that we humans are the culprits.

"Global warming occurs when greenhouse gases generated largely by the burning of fossil fuels like gasoline and coal emit carbon dioxide (CO_2) into the atmosphere. The greenhouse gases encircle our atmosphere and then block the release of infra-red rays thus increasing the earth's temperature. We contribute to the production of greenhouse gases and global warming every time we use our cars. Scary, isn't it?! And this Global Warming leads to Climate Change."

"Can you explain for us exactly what Climate is and how it is different from Weather?" asked Ms. Kaufman.

"I can, Ms. K.", said Fiorella. "Climate is the change or continuity of weather patterns over periods of time. And weather is the conditions at the present. For example, the **climate** may be warming where you live as demonstrated by years of record keeping but today the **weather** might be snowing."

"Very well put, Fiorella!" exclaimed Ms. Kaufman.

"So then," said Reeya, as she continued with the presentation, "the only way to slow the increase of global warming is to refrain from burning dirty fossil fuels and ultimately, end our reliance upon them entirely. We must rapidly move toward the development and application of more sustainable forms of energy consumption such as solar, wind, hydrothermal and biofuel energy and continue researching planet friendly alternative energy systems."

"If we know that we're endangering the future of the entire planet," asked Nikki, "then why aren't we doing all of this more rapidly?"

"That's the question I kept asking myself while researching this," replied Reeya. "The problem is that the dirty fossil fuel industry—oil, gas and coal—have established the energy grid upon which our entire economy is built. It's difficult to turn that ship around and swiftly invest in more planet friendly alternative energy sources overnight."

"It's also true that the dirty fossil fuel industry continues to reap huge profits off of the existing dependency on these 19th and 20th century energy sources." added Fiorella. "So, it's fair to say that they are not quite as motivated to change."

"And that many firms and individuals in the oil, gas and coal industry have, over several decades, spent a considerable amount of their formidable financial resources on questionable research and media ads that call the entire Global Warming/Climate Change issue into doubt," said Reeya. "This disinformation campaign serves to create confusion and doubt in the public's mind and produces climate deniers. They also politicize a scientific issue with campaign donations to elected officials who will then often literally toe the company line and obstruct essential regulatory legislation, and by so doing, shamelessly forsake the future of their own children."

"Sadly true," agreed Antonelli, slowly shaking his head. "We previously mentioned Upton Sinclair. Well, he also said that *'It is difficult to get a man to understand something when his salary depends on his not understanding it.'*

"That, unfortunately, has very much been the case with the issue of climate change and global warming." concluded Antonelli.

"Perhaps the most famous document regarding Earth Day," continued Reeya, "is the 1970 Earth Day Proclamation written by John McConnell which he created for world-wide use and to raise environmental awareness. The document is now located at the United Nations New York Headquarters. The Proclamation underscores McConnell's deeply held belief in the principle of *Unity Through Diversity*. That, although the peoples and cultures of the world are very different in many ways, we can and must come together as a unified voice in protection of our planetary home."

Reeya then posted the following slide on the class power point projector:

Earth Day Proclamation
by John McConnell

June 21, 1970

Whereas: A new world view is emerging; through the eyes of our Astronauts and Cosmonauts we now see our beautiful blue planet as a home for all people, and

Whereas: Planet Earth is facing a grave crisis which only the people of Earth Can resolve, and the delicate balances of nature, essential for our survival, can only be saved through a global effort, involving all of us, and

Whereas: In our shortsightedness we have failed to make provisions for the poor, as well as the rich, to inherit the Earth, and our new enlightenment requires that the disinherited be given a just stake in the Earth and its future –their enthusiastic cooperation is essential if we are to succeed in the great task of Earth renewal, and

Whereas: World equality in economics as well as politics would remove a basic cause of war, and neither Socialism, Communism nor Capitalism in their present forms have realized the potentials of Man for a just society, nor educated Man in the ways of peace and creative love, and

Whereas: Through voluntary action individuals can join with one another in building the Earth in harmony with nature, and promote support thereof by private and government agencies, and

Whereas: Individuals and groups may follow different methods and programs in Earthkeeping and Earth-

building, nevertheless by constant friendly communication with other groups and daily meditation on the meaning of peace and goodwill they will tend more and more to be creative, sensitive, experimental, and flexible in resolving differences with others, and

Whereas: An international EARTH DAY each year can provide a special time to draw people together in appreciation of their mutual home, Planet Earth, and bring a global feeling of community through realization of our deepening desire for life, freedom and love, and our mutual dependence on each other,

Be it Therefore Resolved: That each signer of this People Proclamation will seek to help change Man's terrible course toward catastrophe by searching for activities and projects which in the best judgment of the individual signer will:

• peacefully end the scourge of war...

• provide an opportunity for the children of the disinherited poor to obtain their rightful inheritance in the Earth...

• redirect the energies of industry and society from progress through products...to progress through harmony with Earth's natural systems for improving the quality of life...

That each signer will (his own conscience being his judge) measure his commitment by how much time and money he gives to these purposes, and realizing the great urgency of the task, he will give freely of his time and money to activities and programs he believes will best further these Earth renewal purposes. (At least 9 percent of the world's present income is going to activities that support war and spread pollution. Ten percent can tip the balance for healthy peaceful progress.)

Furthermore, each signer will support and observe EARTH DAY on March 21st. (Vernal Equinox ~~ when night and day are equal throughout the Earth) with reflection and actions that encourage a new respect for Earth with its great potentials for fulfilling Man's highest dreams; and on this day will join at 19:00 Universal Time in a global EARTH HOUR–a silent hour for peace....."

(See original document at: http://www.earthsite.org/proclaim. htm)

"John McConnell's Earth Day Proclamation," continued Fiorella, "was signed by several notable luminaries at the time, including anthropologist Margaret Mead, US Senator Eugene McCarthy and Scientist and Inventor Buckminister Fuller to name but a few."

"So, in conclusion," said Reeya, "Earth Day is not only a celebration of the planet but a somber reminder that we are all stewards of the Earth, responsible for preserving the health and well-being of all creatures and things which inhabit our planetary home...

"And that's our presentation on Earth Day," announced Reeya.

"Great job, Ladies!" exclaimed Ms.Kaufman.

"Wonderful!" declared Mr. Antonelli, applauding and agreeing whole-heartedly with Ms. Kaufman's assessment.

"Any questions?" asked Ms. Kaufman, surveying the class for hands, before nodding toward Tony's upraised palm.

"What I don't understand, Ms. K.," began Tony, "is that if people all over the world are expressing grave concerns about the health of the planet, why haven't we managed to do more about it? Issues like conservation, pollution and especially climate change are very important, so if millions of people are demanding that we take action on behalf of the planet, why are things progressing so slowly?"

"An excellent question" interjected Mike Antonelli. "And I'll be addressing that directly. Right after lunch" he said with a wink.

Ms. Kaufman laughed in agreement, adding "Yes, right after lunch, indeed."

"Thank you all for your informative and thought-provoking presentations. Now, let's enjoy the lovely potluck lunch we've created for ourselves!"

Chapter 5

Lunch: a Multicultural Feast

The class withdrew to the cafeteria anteroom where they eagerly dug into a groaning board table full of foods specially prepared by the students and their parents, reflecting dishes from their individual cultural backgrounds and ancestry. A veritable "United Nations of Cuisine"; the table was covered with delicacies from cultures spanning the globe- including Fiorella's posole and chicken tamales, Nikki's knishes and blintz, Tony's deep dish lasagna and Erin's colcannon and soda bread and, of course, Reeya's delicious khadi and roti with Jamal's scrumptious sweet potato pie making for a delightfully satisfying dessert. A dessert which made everyone almost forget the beautiful "Big Blue Marble" cake baked especially for the occasion.

Many students followed Ms. K's lead and took a slice of Jamal's delicious homemade sweet potato pie back to class to finish off while listening to Mr. Antonelli's long-anticipated speech.

Chapter 6

Mike Antonelli's Earth Day Keynote Address

The class slowly reconvened, as students, many with mouths full and hands laden with plates of second helpings, made their way back to their seats-having both their appetites and cross-culture curiosity sated by the self-created buffet of international cuisine.

Ms. Kaufman spoke briefly with Mr. Antonelli while sipping coffee from her special class mug—a gift from appreciative students. The cup was inscribed with a Chinese proverb: *A teacher for a day is like a parent for a lifetime*. She placed her prized mug delicately on her crowded and cluttered desk, between a stack of papers awaiting correction and a kaleidoscope, another gift from grateful students. Ms. Kaufman then cleared her throat and announced, "And now it gives me great pleasure to introduce this year's Earth Day keynote speaker: teacher, community organizer and social activist, Mr. Mike Antonelli."

Antonelli slowly made his way, amidst polite applause, to Ms. K's podium in front of the class. "What a wonderful repast!" he exclaimed while using his handkerchief as a napkin. "Such a joy to feast upon the fruits of diversity." Your delightfully diverse lunch reminds me of something your school's namesake, Mr. **Cesar Chavez (1927-1993)** said: *'Preservation of one's own culture does not require contempt or disrespect for other cultures.'* And, as you've just experienced, it can also be quite a delicious experience," added Antonelli, with a wink.

"Well, I don't know that I can possibly follow up on such wonderful and well prepared presentations and that delicious lunch, but I'll do my best.

"My name is Mike Antonelli and I've been an educator, community organizer, and social activist since the 1960's. I became active in social justice causes because of two major events of my youth-the civil rights movement led by *Dr. Martin Luther King, Jr. (1929-1968)* and the *Viet Nam War (1955-1975)*.

"I'm not into formal style lecturing and I'm really not here to make a speech but rather to moderate something more like a guided lecture/discussion regarding your wonderful presentations and how they all connect to each other and so very deeply to Earth Day's true meaning. That doesn't mean that I won't be tempted to lecture a bit since I was also, for many years a high school and college teacher much like your wonderful teacher, Ms. Kaufman.

"Okay," taking a deep breath and collecting himself, he continued, "how many of you have heard of a concept known as **Unified Field Theory**? Hands, please." A few widely scattered hands went up as the somewhat perplexed students wondered if this had suddenly become a physics class.

"Yes, you, the lady up back," said Antonelli, pointing at Erin Kelly sitting in the last row. "Please tell us what Unified Field Theory is, if you would."

Erin, who planned on pursuing a career in science and engineering and was awaiting an admissions decision from MIT began, "Well, like much about physics, it's kind of complicated but, put in the most simple terms, I suppose you could say that it's a sort of 'Theory of Everything' that describes, connects and demonstrates the relationship between Fundamental Forces and Elementary Particles."

"Whew! Yeah! That's good enough for our purposes, Erin! Thank you." exclaimed Antonelli. "Don't want to blow everybody's mind with Quantum Theory here! **Science is, indeed, the mind of the human race and Humanities are its conscience.** I'm essentially a wordsmith not a numbers jockey, myself," he chuckled. "Okay," he continued, "so it's helpful for us in Social Studies, to think about it as some force that connects all kinds of activity. An underlying cause of human behavior in all its forms.

"For example, what would you think if I said that all of today's very different presentation topics were actually connected by a kind of social studies Unified Field Theory? " inquired Antonelli.

"I'd say prove it!" shouted Tony as the class laughed nervously.

"Prove it, you say?" Antonelli responded, adding, knowingly "and prove it I shall!

"Let's first list the topics that were presented today", he said picking up a marker and heading toward the whiteboard. "We saw presentations on the plight of labor/the working class, public education and Earth Day. Now, that looks like a pretty disparate collection of topics and issues, so what could possibly be the underlying, 'unifying' force that impacts them and presents a major obstacle to progress for each and every one of them? Anyone care to venture a guess?" asked Antonelli, surveying the class. Seeing nothing but puzzled faces, he provided the answer to his own question. "Capitalism!" he announced. "Predatory capitalism is the single force that influences the development and most often impedes progress in all of these fields of human endeavor."

"Excuse me, Sir," interjected Reeya, "isn't that just politics?"

"Yes and no," responded Antonelli, "Politics is a means by which working people may attain authentic democracy in both government and the workplace. **It's important to remember that capitalism and democracy are not the same; capitalism is an exploitative economic system which benefits capitalists at labor's expense, while democracy is actually a government system that stresses the importance of each citizen having a voice in governing and the decision-making process. Capitalism and Democracy are, in fact antithetical to one another; capitalism is a decidedly undemocratic system that forces workers to obey the orders of capitalists.** If you happen to disagree with me, please feel free to try and use your first amendment rights to free speech with your boss at work and just wait and see how that works out for you," he said, wryly.

"Just politics", continued Antonelli, parroting Reeya with a patient sigh. "There's nothing 'just' or paltry about politics, young lady. It's the means by which we steadily attain a more just society and humane, sustainable planet. And **politics directly impacts every aspect of your personal life.** What's your name?"

"Reeya…..Reeya Patel," she replied.

"Reeya, such a lovely name……so Reeya, do you want to have a future that includes a job? An apartment? Maybe even a home one day? Do you want to have healthcare for when you may be ill and grow old?"

"Yes, of course."

"So since you're not that into politics, let me assure you that your boss and the company that employs you, as well as your landlord and your insurance company are very, very, into politics. And every day they use their political influence to keep your pay low, rents high and to deny you healthcare coverage. So maybe you should think about getting involved in politics if for no other reason than simple self-interest." said Antonelli.

This is a classic example of what the Ancient Greek statesman **Pericles (495-429 BC)** meant when he said: *'Just because you do not take an interest in politics doesn't mean that politics won't take an interest in you.'*

"Can you see that?" asked Antonelli.

Reeya quickly asserted, "I really don't pay much attention to politics. It seems like some kind of bizarre circus to me where nothing really is ever accomplished."

Antonelli thought for a moment then patiently replied "Yes, it can often seem like some kind of bizarre circus, **but politics is the means by which humans sort out their problems and stride toward justice—economic, social, political and environmental justice.**"

Reeya then said, "With all due respect, sir, I, like many of my friends, really pay no attention to politics."

"Isn't this all just some kind of idealistic thinking?" asked Tony.

"Okay let me put it another way then," Antonelli responded. "I believe it was 1960's activist **Abby Hoffman (1936-1989)** who defined government as the institution which decides who steals from who and by how much. So if that's true, wouldn't it make sense to pay attention to, or better yet get involved in politics? If the government is dividing up goodies like tax breaks, healthcare, infrastructure, and education opportunities, shouldn't you be involved in order to better insure that your voice is heard and that you get your fair share?"

"Well yeah, I suppose," Reeya said, cautiously.

"So, contrary to what you and your friends may believe," continued Antonelli, "politics is a very important and, at its best, very noble profession as one dedicates themselves to being a voice for the voiceless—the forgotten people of the working class of all colors and backgrounds who don't have access to the corridors of power enjoyed by the rich and influential. Politics is far too important to be left to the politicians and special interests," concluded Antonelli.

"And as for your charge that this is just some wishful form of idealistic thinking, young man," continued Antonelli, now addressing Tony's remarks. "Yes, from time to time, I've encountered people who make this very criticism. Sometimes, though thankfully not very often, they are, ironically, former students or student-teachers whom I had assisted many years earlier; providing mentoring, guidance, encouragement and writing glowing recommendations for teaching positions or admission to often elite universities that completely transformed their careers and personal lives. They now sometimes, tell me that they are no longer so idealistic, as if this were some kind of fashion trend, like the miniskirt. Like they're just not that into it anymore. I then ask them to consider where they would be today had they not encountered a young, idealistic social studies teacher many years ago when they were anxious, insecure high school or college students desperately seeking relationships, community and careers in what they already painfully understood to be an unjust society. Often times they are simply tired, social activism is emotionally exhausting work and it does take its toll. That's why it's important that cultural workers practice good self-care; healthy diet, exercise, and sleep as well as developing like-minded community. Along with educating ourselves, these are all essentials to well-being and re-charging your batteries for the struggles to come. Indeed, as the great Irish-American labor activist **Mary Harris Jones,** better known as **Mother Jones** (baptized 1837- 1930) said, *'Sit down and read. Educate yourself for the coming conflicts.'*

"However, there are also a very few, an even smaller subset of former students who, having attained personal success with my assistance, believe that they are not indebted in any way to pay it forward. They are often originally from the middle or upper-middle class and find it convenient to forget the idealistic working class teacher they once so eagerly sought out for guidance and mentorship. They haven't forgotten where they came from so much as they've forgotten where *I* came from. And they feel no responsibility to pay it forward.

"As the saying goes," continued Antonelli, "'To those given much, much is expected.' But, hey, that's really not my concern. My willingness to help them speaks to my character and their unwillingness to pay it forward by helping others speaks volumes about theirs.

"As Brazilian Educator and Philosopher, *Paolo Freire (1921-1997)* put it, *'Washing ones hands of the conflict between the powerful and the powerless means to side with the powerful, not to be neutral.'*"

Chapter 7

Capitalism, Communism and Socialism: The Right, The Left and The Center

"Let's begin, then," continued Antonelli, "by defining what Capitalism is and isn't in order to better understand its impact on not only our society but the entire planet."

Antonelli then reached for the classroom copy of the Webster Dictionary and quickly flipped through the pages searching for a definition of capitalism, but was interrupted by Reeya who had quickly called up the Webster Dictionary online with her laptop computer and announced that she had already found the definition. Smiling sheepishly, Antonelli asked her to read it aloud.

Reeya, reading from her laptop screen began, "**Capitalism:** noun. "An economic system based on predominantly private (individual or corporate) investment in and **ownership of the means of production, distribution, and exchange of goods and wealth**; contrasted with socialism or especially communism, in which the state has the predominant role in the economy." (Source: http://www.webster-dictionary.net/definition/capitalism)

"Thank you, Reeya, said Antonelli, "since Webster contrasts capitalism with both communism and socialism, why don't we also take a look at what old Mr. Webster has to say about those two systems as well... If you would, Reeya?"

Reeya called up "Communism" and began reading the definition to the class.

"Communism: noun. 1. A scheme of equalizing the social conditions of life; specifically, a scheme which contemplates the abolition of inequalities in the possession of property, as by distributing all wealth equally to all, or by holding all wealth in common for the equal use and advantage of all." (Source: http://www.webster-dictionary.net/definition/communism)

"And how about the definition of Socialism, please" requested Antonelli. Reeya complied by reading aloud:

"Socialism: noun. A theory or system of social reform which contemplates a complete reconstruction of society, with a more just and equitable distribution of property and labor. In popular usage, the term is often employed to indicate any lawless, revolutionary social scheme." (Source: http://www.webster-dictionary.net/definition/socialism)

"Thank you, Reeya." Antonelli continued, "Yes, indeed. Socialism is often employed to suggest any lawless, revolutionary social scheme. Any scheme that challenges the status quo and the continued exploitation of labor. It is also deliberately conflated with communism and incorrectly viewed as an equally authoritarian system especially by poorly informed workers who unwittingly serve the interests of the ruling class by spreading such drastically misinformed views.

"Well, first off let's examine the language used by Webster in defining these three systems; they first refer to capitalism as an 'economic system' while socialism is called a 'theory' and communism is defined as an outright 'scheme.' That's a classic example of the ruling class controlling the **Dominant Narrative**. Reeya, please find Webster's definition of a **Dominant Narrative**."

"I've already checked," replied Reeya, "and there's no available definition at Webster's website but Wikipedia says that 'a Dominant Narrative can be used to describe the lens through which history is told from the perspective of the dominant culture. This term has been described as an 'invisible hand' that guides reality and perceived reality. Dominant narrative can refer to multiple aspects of life, such as history, politics or different activist groups. Dominant culture is defined as the majority cultural practices of a society. Narrative can be defined as story-telling, either true or imaginary. Pairing these two terms together create the notion of a dominant narrative, that only the majority story is told and therefore heard.'" (Source: https://en.wikipedia.org/wiki/Dominant_narrative#cite_note-onegreenplanet.org-1)

"Thank you," interjected Antonelli, "that will do for our purposes. So let me put it another way; **the dominant narrative promotes the beliefs, values and behaviors of the powerful while the narrative of the powerless goes unheard.** How many of you, for example, have heard the saying that history is written by the victors?" Scanning the class full of raised hands, Antonelli continued, "We gain greater understanding of any culture when we see it through the **lens of powerful vs powerless."**

Jamal, raising his hand, then added, "Yeah, just like the way the history of my people, from slavery to today, isn't covered much in many of our textbooks."

"Exactly," said Antonelli. "Excellent example of a minority story or sub-dominant narrative not being heard and the importance of including ethnic studies in school curriculums such as African-American, Native American, Latinx, Women's, LGBTQ and Labor studies. This should also help you understand where much of the resistance comes from to these programs. Today, despite decades of struggle, the African-American sub-dominant narrative continues to be greatly unheard. From the brutality of slavery to the callous cruelty of Jim Crow Segregation; through the civil rights marches to todays' mass incarcerations, police shootings and brutality towards often unarmed black men, women and even children. This painful past and the more recent brutal examples of two-tier policing inspired the **Black Lives Matter Movement** which has done much to call national attention to this on-going struggle. A struggle only made worse by the mass incarceration motivated in no small part by the expansion of private for-profit prisons."

"The dominant culture does not want to share the narrative with others since it would point out the glaring inequalities put upon minority, poor and working class communities of every kind and more likely further ignite a social movement for justice," interjected Ms. Kaufman. "As a lesbian who teaches history, I, too, find precious little in most conventional history texts about the struggle of LGBTQ (Lesbian, Gay, Bisexual, Transgender and Queer) people's struggle to attain equality in our society. Indeed, there are still school districts in some states where my sexual orientation is considered grounds for dismissal. That is precisely why I include an overview of the struggle for LGBTQ equality in all of my US History courses; from **the Stonewall Rebellion (June 28, 1969)** to **Marriage equality becoming federal law via Obergefell v. Hodges, June 26, 2015.**

"When any people's struggle for justice is marginalized by history and omitted from the national narrative, it serves to diminish them as a group and presents a distorted view of our nation's past and present challenges. It's a matter of power protecting its' privilege from the threat of equality. **Once you start looking at your society through the lens of power relationships you can more clearly see the dominant culture's beliefs, values and behaviors and the ways in which they serve to protect privilege and oppress minorities and the working class.** This is why it's essential to provide public school children with programs that present their unique social narrative. It removes the falsely created stigma of marginalization and provides the student with a more complete understanding of their own ethnic and cultural past so they can make decisions regarding their collective future. Ignorance of one's own past and present oppression only serves the ruling class. It's easier to know where you're going if you know where you've been. 'No root, No fruit', as they say," concluded Ms. Kaufman.

"Couldn't have said it better, myself." said a smiling Antonelli, continuing his presentation.

"As the great African-American writer ***James Baldwin (1924-1987)*** said, *'the victim who is able to articulate the situation of the victim has ceased to be a victim; he or she has become a threat.'*

"That said," continued Antonelli, "returning to our Webster definitions then, isn't it an interesting choice of words to describe Capitalism as an ***economic system*** but refer to Socialism as a ***theory*** and Communism as a ***scheme***?! Very revealing, but only for those with eyes to see, eh?" He chuckled. "And this is the Webster Dictionary, a widely used and highly regarded source of information in schools, colleges, homes and businesses nation-wide. As you can readily see, Webster is, in fact, through connotation, and choice of words, defining either positive or negative feelings toward all three of those systems. So, then, even the dictionary, itself is hardly the objective source of information that it is so often generally considered," Antonelli said to a gobsmacked class.

"And," he continued, "if they can impose the Dominant Narrative in a dictionary, there's no telling where else it may raise its ugly head, hmmm? Like, say, maybe in school textbooks, right?" looking knowingly at Jamal who reflected solemnly while pensively caressing his dreadlocks.

"The Dominant Narrative also influences our vocabulary," Antonelli said. "And thus defines the parameters of public discourse. For example, essential programs for working people like Social Security, Medicare, Medicaid, Unemployment Insurance and the like are referred to as 'Entitlements' as if to say that they are some kind of gift bestowed upon us. Nothing could be further from the truth as we EARN our Social Security by contributing into our account from each and every paycheck during the course of our entire working lives. Another example is referring to hungry people as 'Food Insecure.' Sounds a lot less threatening than 'starving,' right? Insecure might describe your feelings on Prom Night when meeting your girlfriend's parents, but the prospect of starving to death is a considerably more serious condition, isn't it? Today, multiple studies find that twenty percent, approximately one in five children in America live in poverty or should I say 'economic insecurity.'" said a smirking Antonelli. "What did they ever do to deserve to be pawns in this brutal capitalist survival game?

"The side that defines the terminology," continued Antonelli, "always has the advantage. For example the Estate Tax actually affects less than one percent of the very wealthiest people, none the less, the wealthy seek to eliminate it so that they can leave even more money to their already obscenely rich children. Consequently, they refer to it as the 'Death Tax'. A 'Death Tax' implies that EVERYBODY pays this tax when they die which is absolutely not true. As a result of this word play, low-info working class people often think that they are going to be subjected to taxation even en route to the grave! Words have power. The power to persuade, confuse and conflate. That's precisely the purpose of these examples of the Dominant Narrative as employed by the wealthy 2% in order to confuse working people, the 98%, into continuously voting against their own interests.

"So then, what I hope to do during the short time we have together, today is provide you with some background, context and most importantly tools for analyzing your society and best determining the way forward that advances economic, social, political and environmental justice. I call this my **'Conceptual Toolbox'** because you will be provided with a variety of useful tools that will help you to better understand the issues of your day. Now you'll need to be patient with me as I go about this process since it requires a bit of explanation and some of you, especially in this generation of instant gratification, may find yourselves asking 'What's this got to do with Earth Day or even with my life?'

"All I can say is that my experience of teaching this material over many years has confirmed its intrinsic value and that's based on decades of student testimonials to that effect. So then, let's get after it!

"How many of you have seen the movie "The Karate Kid"? (1984 release. https://en.wikipedia.org/wiki/The_Karate_Kid). A smattering of hands go up around the somewhat puzzled student gathering. If you recall the movie, and even if you don't, what happened is that the Kid, Daniel La Russo, went to a karate master named Mr. Miyagi seeking to become his student in order to become a karate master himself. The first thing that Mr. Miyagi does is have Daniel wash his car, instructing him to use alternate sweeping, circular motions with his hands in a 'Wax on. Wax off' pattern," said a gesturing Antonelli.

"Well, after doing this for some time, Daniel becomes impatient and frustrated. He decides to confront Mr. Miyagi about why he is washing his car rather than learning karate. Mr. Miyagi then explains that the sweeping motions of 'Wax on. Wax off' are precisely the essential defensive moves required in karate and a vital fundamental of the martial art. I bring up this early scene from the Karate Kid movie in order to illustrate **the importance of patience and process in the pursuit of knowledge.** You may, like The Kid, question my approach but with patience and perseverance you may not only understand the concepts here but, yourself, become a full-fledged, card carrying social activist Ninja!!" exclaimed Antonelli while striking a karate-like pose to the delight and laughter of Ms. K and the class. "So please consider me a kind of social studies version of Mr. Miyagi," said Antonelli to the chuckling students, "and patiently follow along with what I'm about to present to you."

"Let's begin with some terminology in order that we can better understand each other and effectively communicate what we see when viewing the social-political landscape. Doctors, lawyers, accountants and other professionals have their own terminology and so do social activists." Taking to the whiteboard, Antonelli printed out the word 'Culture' then turned and asked the class if they knew what that meant.

Nikki Sterns raised her hand and said, "Culture is a way of life."

"Very good!" exclaimed Antonelli. "Yes, culture can be defined as a way of life or how people live. But let me give you a more complete and succinct definition." Antonelli began writing on the board: '**Culture is a set of beliefs, values and behaviors shared by a group.**' Stepping back with a certain satisfaction, he continued. "There it is, a definition that describes all cultures from Buddhist monks to the Hell's Angels," he announced, chuckling. "Think about it. All cultures are truly a set of beliefs, values and behaviors shared by a group—whether it's French culture or the Jocks who hang together in the high school cafeteria—they tend to have certain beliefs. For example, the jocks place great value on athletic ability. They value the bond with their team mates and also behave similarly—even wearing the same clothing," he said pointing to Tony's varsity letter football jacket. "So all humans form cultures of one sort or another and establish and follow a certain often unwritten code of beliefs, values and behaviors as members of that culture. What's more, we tend to belong to more than one culture as we also participate in **subcultures—that is a set of beliefs, values and behaviors shared by a smaller group within a larger culture.** For example, some of you perhaps do not speak English, the predominant language of mainstream American culture, when you are at home."

With this, Fiorella quickly raised her hand and volunteered that she, indeed, speaks Spanish when at home with her parents and relatives.

Antonelli approvingly inquired, "And do you celebrate certain holidays, eat special foods and perhaps dress differently as well?"

"Well yes," said Fiorella, "for example we celebrate *Día de los Muertos* or 'Day of the Dead,' from October 31st through November 2nd. It is a holiday in which we Mexicans and Mexican-Americans honor our dead relatives, a bit like Catholic All Soul's Day, I guess. At that time, we build small alters honoring our deceased relatives upon which we will usually place some of their favorite foods. We might also visit cemeteries to be with the souls of our relatives who have passed on and will also leave some of their favorite foods there upon *ofrendas*, altars we build on their gravesites to pay our respects."

"Excellent example, Fiorella," said Antonelli. "And do you prepare and eat any special foods during this holiday?"

"Yes," she replied, "it is common practice to make tamales – both for the living as well as the dead. We also make special sweet cakes for the occasion such as Pan de Muerto (Bread of the dead) and Calaveras, skulls made out of sugar."

"Wonderful!" responded Antonelli. "So there we have but one excellent example of a subculture celebrating a holiday with a clearly defined set of beliefs, values and behaviors within the mainstream American dominant culture. *Gracias*, Fiorella," said Antonelli.

"*Por nada, señor.*" replied a proudly smiling Fiorella.

"And what future plans might such a bright young lady as yourself be setting about next year?" inquired Antonelli.

"I'm not sure," said Fiorella, hesitantly. "You see, I'm a Dreamer. It's a term used for those of us who are part of the Development, Relief and Education for Alien Minors act which never became law. Until recently, I was protected by President Obama's executive order called DACA, (Deferred Action for Childhood Arrivals). I was brought to this country when I was only a very young child. Since President Trump announced that he would end the DACA program, my future, my entire life, is in limbo as I await the official determination of my status and hopefully, some clear pathway to full citizenship. I live each day with the very real threat of being deported from the only country I've ever known." said Fiorella, with a tear running down her cheek.

Antonelli, obviously shaken by Fiorella's situation, attempted to offer his sympathy, "I'm so sorry to hear that, Fiorella. I wish you the best and a quick resolution of your pathway to citizenship." He then wiped his own eyes with the handkerchief he pulled from his well-worn tweed jacket. Gathering himself, he then said, "Immigrants–both documented and undocumented, serve a number of useful purposes for the capitalist class, the

2%. First they do the menial labor that most Americans refuse to do- picking crops, landscaping, etc. They do it at minimum and sub- minimum wages and endure all manner of exploitation such as uncompensated overtime, no benefits or job security and are silenced by the threat of deportation. As labor leader, civil rights activist and your school's namesake, **Cesar Chavez (1927- 1993)** explained, *'The people who pick our food can't afford to eat.'*

"Secondly, these desperate workers serve to drive down the overall wages of all workers and prevents them from organizing into unions. And, finally, the capitalist 2% can demagogue the threat of 'immigrant caravans' and 'invasions' to instill economic and racist fears in the working class. They will claim that these immigrants are 'swarming into the country, taking their jobs and importing crime. It's an old playbook. One that the capitalist 2%, the powerful and privileged, put into play whenever they feel control slipping away.

"So, to continue then," said Antonelli, 'what does the culture concept have to do with our conceptual tool box?' you might ask. Have you considered the possibility that the ruling class and working class participate in two distinctly different cultures? And not only that, but the ruling class uses the cultural diversity of the working class as a tool with which to divide us against each other in order to better control us?

"There's a long, sad history here of divisiveness and hostility. Of whites versus blacks, whites versus browns, yellows and reds, men versus women, straights versus gays, and on and on. All employed and encouraged by the ruling class as wedge issues in order to divide the working class and get us to vote and advocate against our own best interests. More on that as we move along, but in addition to the fact that we all participate in cultures, we are also all susceptible to **Ethnocentrism which is the belief that our**

culture is superior to others. Some forms of ethnocentrism are relatively harmless as in saying that you're culture makes the best food, but others are unspeakably destructive and have indeed caused world wars like Hitler's assertion that the Aryans were the Master Race.

"So then," Antonelli continued, "we've now acknowledged the controlling quality of a **Dominant Narrative** and its impact as well as the existence of many **Subdominant Narratives**. We've also defined three very different economic systems; capitalism, communism and socialism. Now let's continue to build our conceptual toolbox by examining three different economic philosophers from three different centuries and their impact on our culture. Oh, see! There's me using one of our terms- culture-already!!" he exclaimed, laughing.

Chapter 8

Three Influential Thinkers

"For our purposes," Antonelli said, "I will pick up the story of Capitalism with a man who, although not an American, remains, arguably, the biggest single influence on American economic thought. He was an 18th Century Scottish economic philosopher best known for his book, **The Wealth of Nations** published in 1776, the year of the American Revolution. A man named **Adam Smith (1723-1790)**.

"Let's briefly summarize some key elements of Smith's book, which became something of a handbook for capitalists, especially here in the United States. *The Wealth of Nations* is essentially a celebration of capitalism. Smith believed that capitalism could solve many social problems provided certain conditions existed. The first of which is best known by its French name, **Laissez Faire**, which means 'Hands Off.' Smith believed that capitalism thrived when conducted in an environment unregulated by government. He believed that an unregulated **'Free Market'** would more readily lead to what he called the **'Invisible Hand'** which can be defined as self-interest or greed depending on your point of view. Anyway, Smith believed that many of society's problems would naturally be addressed by capitalists who saw gain for themselves as a result of providing a product or service that resolved a problem.

"In order to better illustrate this in its simplest form, let's imagine for a moment that all of us in this class are residents of a village. Our village has a problem, however, in that it is being overrun by mice that spread disease. No one seems to know how to address this serious threat to public health but for arguments sake, the village government stays out of the way and allows individuals to try and resolve it. So, according to Smith, the government of our village has taken a **Laissez Faire or Hands Off** approach which then supposedly, motivates numerous enterprising individuals to work late into the night in their garages seeking to find a solution to the mouse problem. Why? They realize that should they discover the solution- a better mouse trap, they would be rewarded with wealth. This would then be a kind of win-win situation as the village would be rid of the mice and the inventor would be rewarded with wealth. Thus the old saying, 'Build a better mousetrap and the world will beat a path to your door.'" concluded Antonelli.

"So? What's wrong with that?" asked Erin in a somewhat defensive manner.

Antonelli replied, smiling, "Seems like old Adam Smith is right. All we need do is deregulate private enterprise, creating 'Free Markets' and let the 'Invisible Hand' motivate innovations to solve our problems, driven by the prospect of wealth for the innovator.

"Simple, right? Well, maybe not so much. You see, there's a built-in problem with this formula and it's this: there are more than a few essential aspects to a functional society that do not, of themselves, produce a profit for the provider. For example, education is vital to the future of any society but there has been, until recently, a general acknowledgement that this essential task be paid for by the general public at large since we all benefit from a well-educated next generation. Taxes are then collected in order to support a public school system open to all members of the community."

"The same approach should apply to healthcare as well, and does in most of the modern industrialized world except, sadly the United States, where we are still chugging that 'Medicine for Money' Adam Smith 'Free Market' Kool-aide mindset. Consequently in the United States, there are tens of millions of uninsured people who can't afford to see a doctor, countless millions more who are underinsured and a Big Pharmaceutical industry reaping billions of dollars in profits on the sick. In the United States, healthcare is very much a case of your money or your life and the majority of bankruptcies are related to medical expenses." Antonelli explained.

"Meanwhile, virtually all of the western European industrial nations, have some form of centralized, single payer, taxpayer funded healthcare available to everyone because if you live long enough, everyone will eventually need healthcare. This approach, according to numerous studies, provides better results, longer life spans and lower costs than our literally fatally flawed system. The U.S. healthcare sector is, perhaps, the most salient and frankly, barbaric example of the utter failure of the profit driven approach to societal wellbeing.

"Other essential aspects of living in a functional society not well served by Smith's profit motive include transportation, and yes, even housing. Everyone needs a roof over their head but the profit motive turns an essential human need into a commodity in which one might invest, speculate and gain wealth for themselves all while increasing numbers of Americans slip into homelessness or are forced out of downtown locations to make way for condominium developments for rich people. Many of these apartments are then rented at exorbitant rates to those who can afford it or worse yet, lie vacant –only used by the owner during a certain time of year, such as winter condos in Florida," said Antonelli.

"So then, both housing and healthcare become expensive commodities–so much so that we now have vacant housing units amidst rampant homelessness and empty hospital rooms awaiting the arrival of sick insured people who can afford them. All while millions go without and all too often die due to inability to pay a doctor.

"Education, Healthcare and Housing are all glaring examples of the fatal flaws in Adam Smith's Invisible Hand profit driven approach to public policy.

"While some Smith apologists will argue that he would favor government run healthcare, or regulation of banks, etc., there is no doubting the fact that he is a major influence behind America's unrequited love of 'Free Markets'. To this day, Smith's ideas are behind our nation's often inhumane and repeatedly failed attempts to apply a competitive, profit- driven approach to addressing the essential human needs of the young, sick, elderly, poor and homeless.

"So, we now have established Adam Smith as our 18th century capitalist advocate, influencing American economic and social policy from the 1700's to the present. Indeed, the classic American knee-jerk reaction to virtually any societal ill is to seek market based, profit motivated solutions which all too often only worsen the problem as we have seen in the instance of healthcare."

Antonelli then approached the whiteboard again and continued, "Okay, so, now let's turn our attention to another economic philosopher–this one considered by our culture to be more than a tad notorious and that would be **Karl Marx (1818-1883)."**

"Marx looked at the fruit of Smith's Free Market Capitalism some hundred years later and it wasn't a pretty picture; millions of workers struggling for a subsistence living, child labor, squalor, all while the few wealthy capitalists enjoyed the high life. He could readily see with his own eyes that capitalism worked only for the capitalist class while laborers, the vast majority of the population, were demeaned, dehumanized and oppressed. There simply had to be a better way, thought Marx, and in 1848, he published one of the world's most influential pamphlets entitled *'The Communist Manifesto'* in which Marx describes the capitalist-worker relationship and presents a way forward for working people towards a better, brighter, more sustainable future. Marx's writings are often long and make for difficult reading but in this brief pamphlet he provides an excellent working outline of the economic conditions of his time as well as a more viable and just way forward. This brief work includes the now famous, or infamous if you're a capitalist, rallying cry; *'Workers of the world unite, you have nothing to lose but your chains.'* As well as presenting the use of the lens of class struggle when he declares that, *'The history of all hitherto existing society is the history of class struggles.'*

"One of the most important aspects of **The Communist Manifesto** is that Marx first explains his view that **all of history is class struggle**—from the ancient Romans who clearly defined their social classes, rich and poor, as Patricians and Plebeians; through Medieval Society with its Monarchs, Nobility, Peasants and Serfs, and concluding with the 19th century capitalist society in which he lived where workers were engaged in a class struggle against ruthless capitalists who profited from their labor. Marx asserts that the class struggle of his day was simply a continuation of the exploitation of workers under different labels; the ruling class capitalists which Marx refers to as **Bourgeoisie**, versus the working class which he calls the **Proletariat**.

"For simplicity and clarity, I'll refer to them **as Capitalist or Ruling Class vs. the Working Class**. In modern day jargon; the **2 percent** vs. the **98 percent**.

"As Marx saw it, ***control of the means of production*** creates but two classes; The Capitalist Class, a small elite which controls the means of production and the Working Class, the vast majority who must sell their labor and time to the capitalist in order to survive. All other definitions such as middle class, lower class, etc. are nothing more than subdivisions of the Working Class and are often deftly employed by Capitalists to divide workers against each other. The Ruling Class 2% often use race, gender, religion, sexual orientation, immigrant status and the like to instill hatred and distrust and suspicion amongst workers of all kinds in order to better deflect attention and focus away from the real cause of worker exploitation; the capitalist ruling class, themselves.

"We call this tactic **Class Confusion- when a member of the working class mistakenly adopts the beliefs, values and behaviors of the Capitalist Ruling Class.** Examples of this would include members of the working class who support politicians who endorse 'Trickle Down' Economics, union-busting Right-To-Work Laws and oppose Living Wage legislation as well as universal healthcare and investment in public education.

"Perhaps the most important thing Marx did in *The Communist Manifesto*," continued Antonelli, "was to actually define the two primary economic classes. These definitions have become increasingly important in our own time with celebrities and professional athletes making vast sums of money and often mistakenly considered members of the Capitalist/Ruling class: the 2%."

"Here's how Marx defined the elements of the class struggle. First, there was the Capitalist/Ruling class (the 2 percent) and the critical feature of this group is that they ***Control the Means of***

Production, which is the process by which everything is made or produced.

"Ruling class capitalists, the 2 percent," said Antonelli, "control the entire process by which things are made—including the workers, themselves, who actually make the product. **Controlling the means of production means control of the people and the resources necessary to make things.**

"Meanwhile, **the working class, 98 percent, according to Marx, are defined as those who have only their labor to sell in order to survive.** They work for wages and live, as they say, 'by the sweat of their brows.'

"The means of production form the economic basis of a society. More specifically, as Marx points out, **those who control the means of production determine what kind of society we have.**

"In our capitalist society, control of the means of production is held by a small group known as capitalists because they put up capital (money) and purchase the resources, factories and labor needed to produce a given product. Their profit margin is based upon **paying labor less than their actual value** in order to enrich themselves without actually doing any of the work. So what results is a very few people controlling the means of production (ruling class/2 percent) and profiting from the labor of everyone else (working class/98 percent)," concluded Antonelli, pausing to let the concept sink into the students minds as a deafening silence fell over the room.

"In order to more vividly demonstrate this point," he continued, "can you imagine what it would be like to explain capitalism to a visitor from another galaxy?

"Well, you see, Mr. Intergalactic Space-Traveling Dude," Antonelli continued, "here on planet Earth, a very few individuals own everything and for at least forty hours per week, everyone else has to do what they say."

The class roared with laughter at the utter absurdity of a premise they had previously considered 'normal.' They were learning that there is nothing 'normal' about the exploitative nature of capitalism. They would later discover that there is a more humane, sustainable system which has been a demonstrable success in many other nations of the world.

Antonelli then continued, **"Capitalism is the sociopathic idea that the basic necessities of life can be privately owned and that some people are more entitled to food, water, shelter, education and healthcare than others.**

"In sharp contrast to this predatory capitalist model, Karl Marx envisioned a society in which the **workers (labor) themselves controlled the means of production and produced products based not on profits but human needs. The workers would share in the labor and reap the benefits of their work directly through profit sharing.** Instead of the all too familiar capitalist top-down, **vertical organizational model**, decision-making would be made in a **horizontal organizational structure** where every worker had a say in the decision-making process. This would create an industrial and manufacturing workplace based on cooperation rather than competition. Human need, not personal greed

"Remember what I said about the ruling class using our cultural diversity to divide us and make us fight and compete against each other rather than work cooperatively?" Antonelli continued. "They strive through the Dominant Narrative and other tactics to deny workers the ability to fully appreciate that our needs and concerns are far more like those of our black, brown, and gay, brothers and sisters. Cultivation of worker resentment toward their fellow workers, who look different than themselves is essential to ruling class social control. A long time standard capitalist approach is actively cultivating white worker resentment toward workers of color- claiming that black and brown folks are either stealing their jobs or living high off the hog on public assistance programs paid for by THEIR hard earned tax dollars. This has, sadly, been a consistently successful approach and continues to be an open wound in our nation's history- just awaiting the next white demagogue to throw salt in on their way to elected office. Thanks in no small part to the suspicion and resentment created between white and black workers, many whites become angry at the very mention of **'white privilege'** by people of color. They often misunderstand this comment as suggesting that all white folks live lives of luxury. **The term 'white privilege' does not mean that white working class people haven't had a hard and difficult life. It means that the color of their skin isn't one of the things making their lives harder.** This is a classic example of the deliberate divisions of the working class 98% sown by the ruling class 2% in order to maintain power and social control.

"As 19th Century Robber Baron, Jay Gould (1836-1892) put it, *'I can hire one half of the working class to kill the other half.'*

"However, if we organize and work cooperatively, we can make great strides against ruling class oppression and towards a more just society which meets everyone's basic needs. What's required is the cultivation of a **Radical Empathy** for our fellow humans; not blindly accepting the dominant narrative definitions of 'the other' as a threat but viewing them as fellow working people who seek many of the same goals as do we; namely, a living wage, a decent home in which to raise their children, good schools for their kids and a pension sufficient to live out their final years in dignity. We must all begin practicing Radical Empathy when viewing fellow members of the working class who, like ourselves, struggle against the capitalist system. Predatory capitalism is, alas, an equal opportunity oppressor," observed Antonelli.

"Marx's class lens provides us with a powerful tool through which to more accurately assess economies and societies. It's easy to see why a super capitalist society such as ours would make every effort to vilify him since he encourages us to **view our culture in terms of power relationships.**

"So, now," Antonelli said, "let's discuss the work of two 20th century economic philosophers who helped us to better understand, and more importantly apply Marx's concepts to our world.

"During the 20th Century," continued Antonelli, "France produced a prodigious number of notable philosophers who developed a rather complex and sometimes difficult to understand philosophy called **Deconstruction**. Deconstruction can be attributed to several thinkers including **Jacques Derrida (1930-2004)** and **Michel Foucault (1926-1984)**. Let me say, up front, that these guys are most definitely not what you'd call beach reading but I will try my best, at the risk of oversimplification, to boil deconstruction down to its simplest, most basic elements and only for our specific purposes as analysts of society and culture–oh, there's that word again! 'Culture.'" chuckled Antonelli.

"The Deconstructionists," he continued, "provide us with a valuable assessment tool for examining our society."

"What I will present here is a **three step process** we can use to deconstruct virtually any issue, event or policy position; past, present or proposed. So yeah, I'm promising you a lot here so buckle your seatbelts, here we go!"

"In order to make this more tangible, I will, as an example, deconstruct the Federal Government as we walk through the process.

"So now," exclaimed an excited Antonelli, rushing to the board with marker in hand, "here's a three step application of deconstruction as applied to social studies–using the deconstruction of the federal government as an example." He then began frantically marking up Ms K's whiteboard with the following:

Construction, Deconstruction and Reconstruction

Then, remembering that his more tech savvy spouse had provided him with a flash drive of this information to use on Ms. Kaufman's classroom power point, he dug into the pocket of his well-worn tweed jacket, located it and installed it into the projector. Posting the following, he walked the class through the slides.

Step 1. Construction; (to build something) **how an organization is <u>supposed</u> to work; the rules; a blueprint** of the institution's structure and function. **Key phrase; the rules.** An example of the Federal Government viewed through a **constructionist lens** would be to examine the US Constitution. The US Constitution describes the organizational structure, as well as the powers and responsibilities of individual elected officials and provides a statement of our rights as citizens. It describes the requirements for office and responsibilities of various elected officials and the three branches of government. It clearly states that elected officials are supposed to represent the people or the electorate.

Step 2. Deconstruction (to take apart) - This is the key to the process as here we attempt to **take apart** an organization in order to see how money and power maintain themselves. **Key phrase; Follow the money.**

Example of viewing the Federal Government through a deconstruction lens: we quickly discover by following money and power that our government does not actually function in "real time" in the manner described by the constitution. We uncover the existence of an additional layer of power brokers called Lobbyists who pressure elected officials on behalf of money and power in order to win favor for their clients. Indeed some of the most powerful lobbies have in fact managed to determine the legislative agenda- literally deciding what gets to the floor of the House or Senate and what never sees the light of day. One glaring example would be the fact that during the 2009 Obamacare health insurance debate, the widely popular single payer, universal Medicare-For-All proposal was never scored by the Congressional Budget Office (CBO). Scoring is the term for an accounting process conducted by the CBO to determine the cost/ savings related to a piece of legislation. Why was it never scored by CBO? Perhaps because independent studies found that the cost of the Medicare- For- All program was very favorable in sharp contrast to the Obamacare plan. The numbers of people serviced along with the cost effectiveness of universal healthcare would have made this a very difficult plan to reject- which was precisely what the private insurance companies sought to do since Obamacare, unlike Universal Single Payer, pours federal money into the coffers of the private insurers.

Here, Antonelli interjected, "While Obamacare is a significant step forward in addressing our nation's shameful position as the only industrialized western country without universal healthcare, providing healthcare coverage for over 20 million Americans who would otherwise be without any coverage, the program still leaves many millions of people uninsured. Where do you suppose the pressure came from to kick universal coverage to the curb? The people, who by large majorities, favored this approach or the private insurers who would be driven out of business by its enactment? Only by applying Deconstruction and following the money does this in any way make sense. Big Insurance and Big

Pharma said no and the majority of Americans can go pound sand. Doesn't sound much like a democracy does it, now?"

Step 3. Reconstruction- Key Phrase: to rebuild. Perhaps, the most difficult step in the process as we now go about **rebuilding an organization** in a way that provides for economic, social and political justice.

Example of Federal Government being reconstructed would require an initiative to take money out of the political process which would begin with the repeal of the Citizens United case (2010) in which the Supreme Court essentially permitted unlimited and undisclosed donations by corporations and wealthy individuals to the candidates of their choice. This quickly deteriorated into a "cash equals free speech" argument in which the wealthy are guaranteed the bigger megaphone and the poor are silenced. Big Donor driven politics is the reason why legislation that's unpopular with the public often becomes law including the Orwellian titled "Tax Cuts and Jobs Act of 2017" which is a textbook example of the power of big donor cash to drive legislation. The legislation, according to CBO and other studies, is little more than a massive giveaway to the wealthy which blows up the deficit.

It's a textbook example of the impact of big donor money on politics and according to virtually every poll at the time, was widely unpopular with working class Americans who would receive little or no tax relief as the tenets of the bill overwhelmingly favor the wealthy. Perhaps a more accurate title for the bill would be "Christmas comes early for the 2 percent." What's more, the very modest tax cuts for working Americans expire but the hefty cuts for corporations do not.

"Reconstruction is the most challenging aspect of the deconstruction process because it requires action to address injustice- and that often involves protest and yes, Reeya, politics," said a grinning Antonelli, with a playful wink.

"Politics, seen in this context then, is actually an extension of a society's sense of decency; budgets, can and should be viewed as moral documents as they display the priorities of a nation whether it be comforting the comfortable while afflicting the afflicted or addressing the actual needs of working people and the most vulnerable. Does our federal budget reflect the priority of profits or people? Bombs or bread? Private greed or human need? You can learn a lot about a society by examining the priorities it sets forth in its budget. As the great French playwright, **Moliere (1622-1673)** observed, *'It is not only what we do but also what we do not do for which we are accountable.'*

"And while it's sadly true," continued Antonelli, "that government alone can't resolve every ill that plagues society it can certainly make a more vigorous effort to do so. By so doing, government then becomes the dynamic force for progress and social advancement. For example, a law will not stop some individuals from hating black people but it will hopefully, stop them from lynching them which is most definitely a step in the right direction. It took generations to instill deep seated racism into our society and it will likely take generations to fully eradicate it. And, contrary to what the Dominant Narrative may say, racism is not some innate human trait. It's actually culturally learned behavior. Much of it the result of slavery which is, itself, essentially a product of capitalism since it cheapens the cost of labor to zero wages. In order to maintain social control, the slave holding ruling class encouraged white working class folks to look down on blacks in order to distract them from seeing their own exploitation at the hands of the very same slave-owning masters. Unfortunately, they've been effectively using race as a wedge issue for generations in order to divide the working class against itself in order to protect their status and privilege. And I must say that they use it because it, sadly, works.

"President Lyndon Baines Johnson (1908-1973) a southerner, astute practitioner of politics and tireless advocate for numerous civil rights and social welfare legislation explained the white-black working class manipulation this way, *'If you can convince the lowest white man he's better than the best colored man, he won't know you're picking his pocket. Hell, give him someone to look down on and he'll empty his pockets for you.'*

"Or, more simply put, sowing the seeds of class confusion." concluded Antonelli.

"So, now that you understand this very simplified application of the Deconstruction process, you can apply it to virtually any issue or event, past, present or future in order to more clearly see what underlies the motives and intentions of politicians and, more importantly, discover who, exactly, it is that they serve.

"Any questions?" asked Antonelli, surveying the room for hands. Seeing none, he continued.

Chapter 9

The Political Landscape; Right, Left and Beyond

"And now let's take a good hard look at this whole 'political' thing, shall we?" Antonelli said, taking a playful glance at Reeya. "...considering how important it now apparently is," he added with a wink.

"Let's begin with some history here, the whole **'Right vs Left'** and where that came from."

"It is believed that use of the terms 'Right' and 'Left' to describe political leanings has its origins in the French Revolution of 1789 when the National Assembly became divided into two groups: Supporters of the King (conservatives) sat on the right and supporters of the revolution (liberals) sat on the left side of the chamber. Today, these terms are used widely in political science to describe politicians and policies. The present Red-Blue color code-Republicans/Right being Red and the Democrats/Left being Blue was something that the television networks created during the 2000 Presidential election.

"Generally speaking, today, **The Right (Conservatives, Re-**

publicans, neoliberals) supports authority, hierarchy, social order and tradition while **The Left subscribes to equality, egalitarianism and the removal of power relationships which are oppressive in a social, economic or political context.**

"What does that all mean in terms of political parties across the spectrum?" Antonelli asked nobody in particular as he grabbed a marker and headed back to the projector. "Well, let's examine a diagram of a political flow chart which identifies and defines the major political perspectives.

"For convenience sake," continued Antonelli, "we will examine our chart from right to left since the Right kinda starts the whole process and other perspectives are essentially reactions to it and its beliefs and tenets." He then posted the following slides:

The Right: Essentially comprises today's Republican Party in the United States, and believes in the established social order. They are suspicious, indeed, often threatened by the idea of social change. They are advocates of the status quo and often harbor a deep distrust of people's ability to manifest more egalitarian social relationships, especially in the workplace. They are generally, admirers of tradition and view institutions like churches, as well as a very narrow (strict constructionist) interpretation of the constitution as vital aspects of social cohesion. Two additional, still more extreme versions of this conservative, pro-capitalism view are **Libertarianism and Fascism.**

Libertarians claim that the source of all our societal ills is the government itself; that we would be better off without the 'tethers of government interference,' aka regulation and legislation.

"So if you believe that we'd be a better society without civil rights laws and food and drug inspection then Libertarianism might just be right for you," explained Antonelli. "Imagine, for a moment what this Libertarian Utopia would look like? Without government playing referee—protecting minority, worker and women's rights we would devolve into a survival of the fittest/richest state where the strong and powerful dominate and fully exploit the vulnerable, unchecked. Do you trust the meat industry to insure that your barbeque is not a salmonella feast? or would you feel more comfortable having a trained government official declare your meat safe to eat? It always kills me when I see state college students supporting some Republican claiming to be a Libertarian. The poor fools don't seem to understand that if Libertarians had their way, government funded schools and universities would be a thing of the past. Talk about class confusion, eh?!" exclaimed Antonelli, smacking his head and laughing.

"Next time you should happen upon a Libertarian, ask them to cite an example of a society that is thriving under such a Draconian philosophy—and don't hold your breath waiting for a response. You're most likely going to hear some talking point claptrap regarding 'Freedom', 'Liberty' and 'rugged individualism'. Which translates into freedom from healthcare, liberty from public education and a rugged individual's right to work for subsistence wages. More naïve individuals may be attracted to this social theory because of their pro-marijuana position without fully understanding that many Libertarians also don't believe that the government should regulate <u>ANY</u> drug.

"The best example of a society resulting from this cruel, oppressive and compassionless philosophy," continued Antonelli, "might be seen in William Golding's classic novel, *'Lord of the Flies'* (1954) where the strong are unrestrained in exploiting the vulnerable. Bottom line; **the ultimate objective of Libertarianism is the complete privatization of power.**

"And if Libertarianism isn't oppressive enough for you, we have Fascism – AKA; capitalism on steroids. Fascism is the most severe of right wing political philosophies and generally thrives when capitalism encounters one of its many cyclical failings such as high unemployment or economic depression. Its base, fervent, appeal is to our darker emotions and destructive passions such as nationalism and tribalism, fomenting a twisted populism that celebrates nation and usually race over the individual and self-expression. **Fascism is an authoritarian political philosophy characterized by an oppressive, dictatorial ruler, regimental control of industries, suppression of individual rights such as free speech and submission of one's self to the greater good of the homeland—extreme patriotism devolving into outright jingoism, usually including an aggressive foreign policy.** Thus giving new meaning to **Dr. Samuel Johnson's (1709-1784)** astute observation that *'Patriotism is the last refuge of scoundrels.'*

"An excellent definition of fascism" said Antonelli, "often attributed to Italian Fascist Dictator **Benito Mussolini (1883-1945)** is, *'Fascism should more properly be called corporatism, since it is the merger of state and corporate power.'*

"The essential tenets of Fascism: blind devotion to country and corporatism, make it more amenable to wars. So then, Libertarianism and Fascism represent two more severe forms of right wing, conservative politics.

"Since conservative, right wing ideology protects the property and privilege of the ruling class," Antonelli continued, "it should come, then, as no surprise that many wealthy individuals and families subscribe to a conservative philosophy. Since the present state of affairs does, indeed, work quite well for them, despite the suffering it places upon the majority, they are not personally motivated to support any social change. Indeed, historically, one would be hard pressed to point to any major advancement in economic, social or political justice attributable directly to conservatives or their beliefs. Since the present exploitative economic and political system works for them, they support and serve as apologists for the status quo; attempting to justify, however illogically, the unjustifiable and the suffering of the majority be damned. **Consequently, conservatives are far more likely to be change obstacles than change agents.**

"Alas, since so many conservatives are financially well off, it only serves to follow that they would be strident defenders of and apologists for the status quo. Continuous attempts by the well -heeled conservative class to defend such an obviously indefensible social order often make more than a few look quite stupid indeed. They are simply attempting to justify a position which benefits themselves and their privileged place on the economic food chain.

"As Harvard Philosopher **John Rawls (1921-2002)**, succinctly put it, *'Where you stand* (on socio-economic policies*) depends on where you sit.'* (On the economic food chain)."

"But aren't there also many conservatives who are not wealthy or come from working class backgrounds as well?" asked Tony. "How do you explain this?"

"So glad you asked," replied a grinning Antonelli, "because that leads us to a discussion of a sadly, all too common phenomenon called **'Class Confusion.'**

"Class Confusion can be described as a condition in which a person endorses and supports the beliefs, values and behaviors of a class other than their own, usually to their own detriment. It is a condition most often experienced by working class people who believe the Ruling Classes Dominant Narrative about this country being a great meritocracy in which everyone gets what they earn through hard work and that those with the most deserve it because they worked harder or were smarter than others. Of course, nothing could be further from the truth since some of the hardest working people in our culture- the working poor, often hold two and three jobs and can barely make ends meet. If the ruling class myth about those who work hardest , rightfully, have the most were, true, then fast food workers, janitors and other service sector employees would be unimaginably wealthy!" explained Antonelli, laughing at the absurdity of the notion.

"Does class confusion ever occur amongst the rich?" asked Fiorella.

Antonelli considered the question for a moment then replied, "Well, class confusion is, indeed, far more common amongst working class people since they are the target of the Dominant Narrative designed to make them blame themselves for their own precarious condition- and not realize that their position in the socio-economic hierarchy is largely a product of design called **Structural Poverty**. In order for the few to have so much and be considered 'winners' it's necessary for there to be a large and ever growing number of poor 'losers' who blame themselves for their condition in order to better insure that they won't unite and rise up against their true oppressors—the wealthy 2%. But, to answer your question, Fiorella, sometimes but not often enough, a person of wealth suffers from what might be called class confusion and is considered a traitor to his class such as Presidents Teddy and Franklin Roosevelt. Both of whom made great strides on behalf of working people.

"In contrast to conservatives who revere authority and admire tradition and property rights, **The Left (Liberals/Progressives**) generally, today's **Democratic Party**, believe in human equality and progress through social change often driven by government legislation." Antonelli said.

"However, it's critically important to remember that Liberals, like

Conservatives, also believe in the capitalist system and only seek to use government programs and regulation as a means to 'buff the rough edges off' of capitalism. Their goal is not the complete elimination of the barbaric, exploitative Capitalist system but to somehow, through legislation and regulation, change its evil ways, despite its tawdry history. **Liberals believe that Predatory Capitalism can be redeemed and reformed.**"

Jamal then raised his hand and asked, "How can a system that makes the capitalist the absolute master and workers his servants and slaves ever truly be salvaged?"

"Great question!" an excited Antonelli replied. "That's precisely why Democratic Socialism stresses the importance of expanding democracy to the workplace so that those who actually do the labor and produce the product have a say in policies and procedures directly impacting them. For many, the fundamentally undemocratic nature of predatory capitalism renders any attempt at redemption little more than a fool's errand. Reminds me of dozens of old country songs about good hearted women trying to change good timing men," said a smiling Antonelli. "How does that usually work out for them? Kind of like putting lipstick on a pig?! Right?"

"And while it is true that virtually every attempt to improve the lot of the working classes from the 1930's until today is a result of liberal Democratic Party philosophy–programs such as Social Security, Medicare, Medicaid, Minimum Wage Laws, and Unemployment Insurance. It's also true that these programs often fall woefully short of providing the comprehensive assistance needed. All too often, a hard won government program heralded as a panacea for one of the many ills besetting the working class turns out to be more akin to putting a bandaid over cancer. The cancer being predatory capitalism. These policies are, also, often vehemently opposed by the Conservative Right/Republicans who, over time, frequently manage to find ways to repeal whatever little assistance these Liberal measures may have provided. And, thus the vicious cycle of baby-step Democratic progress followed by Republican repeal. The only certainty is that the real needs of working class people are never heard nor sufficiently addressed.

"What's worse still, is that over the past few decades we have seen the Republican Party move even further to the Right and the Democrats follow them in desperate and often futile attempts to create bipartisan legislation. This process, called **Asymmetric Polarization, where one party moves toward its extreme polarity and the other chases them, has left the working class without a major voice in the political process.** Combine this with the fact that in the age of 'Citizen's United,' money doesn't talk, it screams and BOTH parties are seeking essentially the same donors with the same capitalist agendas which then leaves the 98% of Americans without a major political party advocating on their behalf. This has resulted in so-called 'Democrats' agreeing to more restrictions on welfare, deportation of immigrants, unjust trade agreements like NAFTA and even bank deregulation. Despite this betrayal of workers by the Democratic Party, labor continues to support them since the only alternative, the Republicans, have moved from vehemently hostile to, at times, utterly unhinged in their war against workers, women, minorities and labor. So with Democrats like this, who needs Republicans?" Antonelli rhetorically inquired.

"So then, let's never forget, that **both major political parties endorse and support capitalism**, and consequently, they, alas, have far too much in common. As turn of the 20th century American labor leader **Eugene V. Debs (1855-1926)** said, *'The Republican and Democratic parties, or to be more exact, the Republican-Democratic party, represent the capitalist class in the class struggle. They are the political wings of the capitalist system and such differences* *as arise between them relate to spoils and not to principles.'*

"However, it's also important to note that there are substantial differences as well," noted Antonelli. "Let's not fall prey to false equivalencies: the two political parties are not equally destructive. As I've previously mentioned, the Democrats provided virtually every social safety net program ever enacted by the federal government; from social security to Medicare, Medicaid, minimum wage and unemployment insurance laws, as well as laws protecting women, children and the LGBTQ community. Not to mention the Affordable Care Act (aka Obamacare) and the DACA program, designed to protect 'Dreamers;' immigrants who were brought here as children, have known no other culture but ours and did not personally choose to break any immigration laws."

"Meanwhile, history teaches us that all of these programs have been vehemently opposed by the Republican Party which ceaselessly attempts to cut or repeal many of them to this very day. So let us not be deceived by this kind of 'curse upon both your houses' mentality," warned Antonelli. "It only serves to muddy the waters and provide political cover for much of the unconscionable conduct of Republicans. After all it was a Republican who, in 2016, denied a Democratic president his constitutional right and responsibility to nominate and attain a vote on his selection for the Supreme Court. Senate Leader, Republican Mitch McConnell, did precisely that for nearly one full year until Republican President Donald Trump won a questionable and controversial election and appointed a conservative justice to the 'stolen seat.'" Antonelli said.

"In this instance one might be forgiven for thinking that the (R) after McConnell's name stands for Ruthless. **A still easier way to remember the difference between Republicans and Democrats is that it's like driving a car; if you want to**

move forward you put the car in 'D' for Democrat. And if you wish to go backwards you shift into 'R' for Republican." explained Antonelli.

"The challenge for most progressives and democratic socialists is this: do we attempt to co-opt the Democratic Party and return it to its traditional role as advocate for the working class or do we set out on our own in creating a third party to challenge the two pro-capitalist party establishment? History has not been kind to third party initiatives," observed Antonelli, "and in the age of Citizens United, the political parties often serve as little more than cash registers, so it's not an easy question to resolve. Perhaps the way forward is to do both simultaneously. We can work to enlist and promote truly progressive and even democratic socialist candidates within the Democratic Party and also use those same grassroots methods to build up a consensus for a third party approach which can then be used to threaten corporate establishment Democrats in order to keep them honest. All of this would serve to educate the public about the many benefits of democratic socialism and help transform public consciousness as it did with recycling and Earth Day.

"What we must avoid," warned Antonelli, "is creating divisive litmus tests amongst progressives that only serve to weaken the people's movement and further empower the capitalist class. History teaches us that progressives are very good at creating circular firing squads. The stakes are far too high now to risk losing an election to a right wing capitalist because we don't entirely agree with every position held by the more progressive, or indeed, less destructive, candidate. We must remember that we are electing a human being, not a saint and never allow the perfect to become the enemy of the good" concluded Antonelli.

Chapter 10

Americans Taste Democratic Socialism. And Like it.

Antonelli, further considering Fiorella's excellent question regarding class confusion and the rich, continued, "I suppose that you could say that a kind of class confusion occasionally but, alas all too rarely, afflicts some members of the ruling class and they are then often capable of pulling the levers of power in order to provide some bit of justice for the working class. Such a person was **President Franklin D. Roosevelt (1882-1945)**. Although a child of wealth and privilege, FDR, perhaps motivated by the wide spread suffering of working people during The Great Depression (1929-1941) , established a good deal of what passes today for a social safety net in our country from Social Security to unemployment insurance to minimum wage laws. In fact, one could accurately claim that FDR was our first Democratic Socialist president and his policies were designed to assist working people and the most vulnerable. This was a dramatic change from previous presidents who, all too often, were little more than rubber stamps for legislation supporting the corporate ruling class and their relentless exploitation of people and insatiable quest for greater profits.

"Then there's also the case of President Lyndon B. Johnson, a product of the working class with great political skills who rose to the national stage as President John F. Kennedy's vice president. Johnson became president as a result of Kennedy's assassination in 1963. A former school teacher who never forgot where he came from, LBJ's Great Society program created a multi-faceted 'War on Poverty' which included the creation of Medicare and Medicaid providing healthcare to the elderly and poor. I still have vivid memories of visiting the LBJ Presidential Library in Austin, Texas and standing before an exhibit listing his many legislative achievements and social programs. I recall the tears running down my cheeks as I looked upon his accomplishments, realizing full well that without his work, I would not likely have ever escaped from poverty, myself," recalled a visibly moved Antonelli.

"FDR and his New Deal policies were essentially America's first incremental taste of Democratic Socialism," continued Antonelli, attempting to pull himself together. "And America very much liked what they saw. In fact they liked it so much that they elected FDR to an unprecedented and never to be repeated four terms as President. Contrary to the claims of some conservatives, Democratic Socialism is not some foreign ideology being imposed upon the American people. It's a natural and very essential curbing and attenuation of capitalism's exploitative essence and it has never been a stranger to our shores.

"No less a thinker than **Albert Einstein (1879-1955)**, another famous Democratic Socialist, explained it best, *'The real purpose of socialism is precisely to overcome and advance beyond the predatory phase of human development.'*

"Unfortunately, the Right, fearful that the slippery slope they had long dreaded was happening–that is, having experienced a wee bit of FDR's New Deal Democratic Socialist policies, the working class would demand more—made every effort to obstruct New Deal initiatives. Consequently, conservatives have long objected to and sought to repeal FDR's efforts to provide a better quality of life, a New Deal, for working people. The wealthy called Roosevelt a 'traitor to his class', and he, indeed was. One who was rewarded for his class 'betrayal' by appreciative American workers, the elderly and the poor, who, as I mentioned, elected him to an unprecedented four terms as President of the United States."

"Why do so many conservatives keep trying to repeal programs that help working people and the poor?" asked Fiorella.

"**Dogma**," replied Antonelli, "pure dogma as well as simple greed. You know what dogma is, right? **Dogma is a prescribed doctrine or belief that must be accepted without questioning—even despite all evidence to the contrary.** Conservatives essentially believe that helping working people is not the role or function of the government. They subscribe to 'Limited Government' and it's why they so resent paying taxes and abiding by industrial and environmental regulations. They believe that taxes are a form of tyranny and 'theft' and that private charities are the correct way to help the less fortunate.

"Yet, ironically," Antonelli continued, "Americans of all classes including the ruling class, flock each Holiday season to see renditions of Charles Dicken's classic statement against ruling class cruelty called 'A *Christmas Carol*' in which the protagonist; miserly business owner Ebenezer Scrooge, is asked to donate on behalf of the poor and destitute to which he replies, 'Are there no workhouses? Are there no prisons?' In other words, 'to hell with the poor and most vulnerable.'

"The widespread popularity of Dicken's work is based on the deeply held human desire for redemption and we are delighted and comforted by Scrooge's transformation from miserly businessman to charitable, caring human being. It gives us hope that all such cruel, compassionless, capitalists may, one day, find redemption and help relieve the suffering of the poor. It's a wonderful fairy tale," said Antonelli, "but let's remember that it took supernatural forces to 'scare the Dickens' out of Scrooge and transform him from selfishly stingy capitalist to a compassionate human being. We simply can't afford to wait for the return of the Ghosts of Christmas Past, Present and Future to redeem the 2% who are exploiting people and planet. That's the rightful purpose of Democratic Socialism."

Chapter 11

Economic Policies; Republican and Democratic

"So now, let's take a look at both major political party's economic policies, shall we?" said Antonelli.

"First, the Republicans/Conservatives, who continue to subscribe to a repeatedly failed economic theory called **'Supply Side' Economics**–often referred to as **'Trickle Down' Economics** since they claim that tax benefits to the wealthy will trickle down onto the working classes which unfortunately has never, historically, been the case. For this very reason, Republican **President George H.W. Bush (1924-2018),** in an unusual fit of candor, once described it as 'Voodoo Economics'. And that it truly is," added Antonelli, "especially, if you were paying attention during our discussion of how capitalism literally rewards those who most effectively exploit labor."

"Anyway, according to Conservative Republican economic dogma, the best way to stimulate and energize the economy is by giving large tax breaks to the wealthy as this will provide them with surplus capital with which to invest in plant upgrades and, supposedly increase pay and create more jobs. They mistakenly and deliberately view the wealthy as the 'Job Creators.' All that needs to be done, according to Supply Side advocates, is motivate the wealthy classes by sweetening the pot with huge tax breaks and deregulation of business and, viola!, job creation will become an epidemic and the economy will soar, so they claim.

"However history tells us a very different story," Antonelli said, "On repeated occasions, hefty tax breaks have been extended to the wealthy at the expense of funding critical programs for the working class, with virtually no impact on job creation or wage increases. 'How can that be,' you ask? Remember the essential premise of capitalism is to devalue labor in order to maximize profit. So instead of improving facilities, raising worker pay and hiring new employees, these fat cats simply pocket the tax cuts as a bonus for themselves, and their stockholders and, in too many cases, use the money to help cut expenses for outsourcing their businesses overseas in order to better exploit lower wage workers and conduct business with still fewer regulatory restraints.

"Yet another result of this catastrophic policy is that it further depletes available government funds for essential programs for the working class such as Social Security, Medicare, Medicaid, Head Start, WIC and CHIP. The huge, self-inflicted, deficit created by handing over precious tax dollars to the wealthy then becomes the excuse for budget austerity by the ruling class 2%, who then seek to cut vital social programs for the working class 98%. It's actually ruling class warfare against workers disguised as an economic policy and it's an, historically proven, failure.

"As **President Lyndon B. Johnson (1908-1973)** put it: *'Republicans simply don't know how to manage the economy. They're so busy operating the Trickle-Down Theory, giving the richest corporations the biggest break; that the whole thing goes to hell in a hand-basket.'*

"Republican Supply Side/Trickle-Down Economics reminds me of my days growing up on the wrong side of the tracks," Antonelli recalled. "Some folks would pull a 'Chew and Screw'. A chew and screw is when you eat a meal in a restaurant and run off without paying the bill. Republicans and their wealthy patrons repeatedly feast on big tax breaks then run off without paying their workers a fair share of the money to which they are rightfully entitled.

"Thankfully," continued Antonelli, "these repeatedly failed Republican policies are a tougher sell to the nation's soon to be new demographic majority–women, people of color and youth. They seem to more readily see the scam of tax giveaways to the wealthy for what it is and better understand that it comes at a cost to them in cuts to essential working class programs like education and infrastructure. Consequently, in response to their ever-dwindling popularity, the 'Party of Lincoln' has more recently resorted to gerrymandering districts and creating daunting gauntlets of voter suppression in order to maintain power and control. Morally malnourished and ideationally bankrupt, if old Abe Lincoln, The Great Emancipator, could see what's happened to his Republican Party today, he'd never stop vomiting.

"On the other hand, we have the **Democratic/Liberal economic policy** called **Keynesian Economics aka 'Percolator Economics'**, named after British economist **John Maynard Keynes (1883-1946). Keynes theory correctly surmised that the <u>REAL</u> job creator is in fact, not wealthy capitalists, but <u>consumer demand</u>.** And that the fastest and most effective way to stimulate an economy is to provide big tax cuts for the middle and working classes – **not** the wealthy class. With extra money in their pockets, the working class will buy stuff; cars, TVs, furniture, and even dine out more often thus creating demand for more employees across all sectors of the economy. This approach has worked with remarkable results beginning with its implementation by President Franklin D. Roosevelt to thwart the Great Depression of the 1930's and was also used by President Barack Obama to slay the Bush Crash of '08. When combined with government funded infrastructure projects it's not only a major job creation mechanism but the path to an upgraded national transit, water and power grid. In each case, despite Republican objections and, especially in the case of Obama, unprecedented Republican obstruction based in no small part on racism towards America's first black president, the policy has worked. Now it could have worked even more effectively were it not necessary to appease business/corporate interests by giving them a share of the tax cuts which of course, most did not invest in plant upgrades or hiring during an economic downturn.

"It's also important to note that in both instances, Democratic Presidents Roosevelt and Obama successfully employed Keynesian economic policies in order to clean up economic disasters created by their Republican predecessors who caused the catastrophes via 'Trickle Down' economic policies, deregulation and small government, 'starve the beast' (government) defunding of social programs designed to help working people. Modern history certainly demonstrates the truth behind the slogan 'The Democratic Party: Mopping up Republican messes since 1933.'"

"And so," concluded Antonelli, "we then have our sad political/ economic landscape, friends. One election brings into power a Republican administration, which attempts to successfully live up to its reputation as the 'handmaidens of the boardroom,' the party that comforts the comfortable while afflicting the afflicted; slashes taxes on those most able to pay while attempting to 'starve the beast' of government, making it 'small enough to drown in a bath tub,' as they like to say. This, of course, inevitably leads to either a recession or worse yet, a full throttle economic meltdown. At which time, the electorate comes to its collective senses, if only momentarily, and elects a Democratic administration to turn our ship of state back off the economic precipice by implementing the tried and true precepts of Keynesian economics. As British Prime Minister **Winston Churchill (1874-1965)** observed, *"You can always count on Americans to do the right thing...after they've tried everything else."*

Chapter 12

One Step Forward, Two Steps Back

"This vicious cycle of political struggle, of one step forward, two steps back," continued Antonelli, "usually finds us ringing bells of celebration for some new social program one day, only to be wringing our hands in exasperation on the next as it's repealed by Republicans. Sad to say that this Conservative vs Liberal, Republican vs Democrat merry go round is pretty much the state of affairs, historically, and a pretty fair overview of the present American political landscape. The injection of big money into politics boosted by court decisions like **Citizens United (2010)**, only serves to further advance the agenda of the ruling class 2% as they can now essentially purchase politicians from either side of the aisle as best serves their purposes. As a result, the two political parties today, often serve as little more than cash registers raising money for increasingly expensive campaigns between the 'lesser of two evils' candidates both of whom are often beholden to wealthy capitalist donors. Consumer advocate and presidential candidate **Ralph Nader (1934-Present)** was all too accurate when he said that *'The only difference between the Republican and Democratic parties is the velocities* *with which their knees hit the floor when corporations knock on their door.'*

"History provides an excellent example of this 'one step forward, two steps back' vicious cycle during the all too brief **Progressive Era (1890-1916)**, when liberals, led largely by women such as **Jane Addams (1860-1935), Grace (1878-1939) and Edith (1876-1957) Abbott and Sophonisba Breckenridge (1866-1948)** directed ambitious projects including **Hull House in Chicago**, the first settlement house in the United States that addressed the needs of the urban poor, immigrants and children. They provided physical assistance as well as vocational training and advocated against child labor in response to the cruelty and barbaric exploitation of workers during the **Gilded Age of Robber Barons (1870-1895)**. This was during the brutal years when **Rockefeller, Carnegie and Morgan,** established themselves as **America's Ruling Class**.

"These brave and compassionate women," continued Antonelli, "along with leaders of the **Women's Suffrage Movement**, including **Susan B. Anthony (1820-1906) and Elizabeth Cady Stanton (1815-1902),** worked to alleviate the brutality of predatory capitalism and to get women the right to vote. Some great strides were made during this period as Progressives used government laws and regulations to address the cruel consequences of Gilded Age 'free market' capitalism. Another women, an African-American from the south, **Ida B. Wells (1862-1931),** collected data and called national attention to the all too common practice of lynching blacks and described how this practice was employed in the south to intimidate and oppress the black community. Born into slavery, Wells was one of the founders of the **National Association for the Advancement of Colored People (NAACP)** in 1909 and an inspiration to women activists from every background.

"During this **Progressive Era, (1890-1920)** writers, called **Muckrakers** exposed corporate corruption and abuses and **Upton Sinclair's** book, **'The Jungle'** (1904) described in gory detail the inhumane working conditions and lack of sanitation practices in the meat packing industry leading to the passage of the Pure Food and Drug Act in 1906, the first regulatory law established by the federal government upon an industry.

"The Progressives were, indeed, truly progressive", concluded Antonelli, "and some great strides were made for workers, women, children and immigrants during that period. However, these advances were short lived since, with the coming of World War I, the nation's attention and resources shifted to events in Europe essentially taking the national spotlight off of progressive domestic issues. The war served as a useful distraction for the ruling class after 1914 and social progress was essentially, stifled. Again, one step forward, two steps back. By revealing the ghastly living conditions of workers, especially children, Progressives and Muckrakers were, however, able to apply enough social pressure upon the 2% ruling class to compel them to provide some explanation and justification, however feeble, for the appalling living conditions under which so many workers subsisted while the Robber Baron's lived lives of luxury and conspicuous consumption."

Chapter 13

Social Darwinism: Justifying the Unjustifiable

"The modern conservative is engaged in one of man's oldest exercises in moral philosophy. That is, the search for a superior moral justification for selfishness." John Kenneth Galbriath, (1908-2006) Harvard Economist and Kennedy Administration Advisor

"Prior to the outbreak of World War I," said Antonelli, "there was increasing public pressure from Progressives, supported by a steady stream of scandals exposed by Muckrakers, upon the ruling class to provide some kind of justification for the widespread economic inequality. 'Why was it considered okay,' asked progressives, 'that ruling class individuals enjoyed luxury and abundance while millions suffered and subsisted?' Progressives and the public increasingly demanded an explanation and justification for the vast chasm of economic inequality. But how to go about justifying the morally unjustifiable? The capitalists would find their answer in a pseudo-scientific theory expounded by two professors, Herbert Spencer in Britain and William Graham Sumner in the United States.

"Spenser and Sumner," said Antonelli, "would promote a social perversion of biologist Charles Darwin's (1809-1882) renowned theory of evolution and declare that *'survival of the fittest'* also applied to the world of humans. Wealth, according to Spenser and Sumner, was evidence of one's 'fitness'. The wealthy were the fittest members of society, more evolved than others and economic inequality was simply a matter of human 'evolution.' The poor, were considered unfit and best left to die off in order to further advance human development, evolution and progress. Economic injustice, they argued was a matter of genetic superiority and attempts to assist the poor were futile and only served to delay human progress.

"This fraudulent and immoral theory resonated with the Zeitgeist of the Industrial Age. In her presentation earlier, Reeya had referred to the concept of Zeitgeist or 'Spirit of the Times.' Social Darwinism presented itself as another 'scientific' theory in an age of scientific and industrial progress.

"Let me expand a bit about the Zeitgeist concept," continued Antonelli. "Societies, all societies, tend to become fixated by certain events during different times. When closely examined, we can almost breakdown the zeitgeist based on decades. For example, the Zeitgeist of the 1960's in America was Vietnam, Civil Rights and the Hippie Counterculture. During the 1980's the culture's zeitgeist focused on Yuppies, 'Beemers' and cocaine. The same decade-to-decade focus can be traced by individual life experience too. For example, when I was in my twenties, my focus–and that of my buddies–was girls and dating; in my thirties, we were all caught up in activities with our kids, little league, school dance presentations and the like; our forties were spent career climbing, becoming department heads or getting that corner office; and our fifties were pretty much spent talking about our prostate health," he said, chuckling. "You'll discover this personal zeitgeist thing once you've lived for a while. And remember that the same is true for the greater society in that each decade seems to bring a new and different focus. Anyway, Social Darwinism hit the zeitgeist sweet spot with a culture enthralled with scientific discovery and industrial innovations."

"We cannot overstate the impact of Social Darwinism on American society. While widely discredited today, its basic principles still play a major role in the beliefs, values and behaviors of American culture and how we view social classes, especially amongst Republicans/conservatives."

Antonelli, quickly moved towards the power point projector and posted the following slides:

Social Darwinism impacts our culture in four destructive ways;

1. **Belief that the rich are special.** A different breed of human; more intelligent and capable and thus more entitled than others. We see this worship of the wealthy in media in the form of magazines like *People*, and *US* as well as TV programs detailing the lifestyles of the rich and famous. This belief also leads to the misconception, encouraged by capitalists, that only the wealthy are fit to serve as government leaders. You'll often hear wealthy political candidates charge their opponents with "having never met a payroll", suggesting that only successful business leaders have the chops to govern when, fact is, nothing could be further from the truth. Fun Fact: Only two US Presidents have had business backgrounds and degrees: George W. Bush and Donald J. Trump. I'll let you compare their respective accomplishments and debate which was more destructive. But I will note that the Great Economic Crash of '08 occurred on the watch of MBA-Harvard Business School degree holder George W. Bush.

2. **The poor are unfit**. There's no use trying to help these people, the wealthy claimed. The poor, they said, were simply genetically inferior. This became a useful talking point for conservatives when pressed about assisting the poor. It had nothing to do with economics they claimed, it was about "science". This reference to "science", however bogus, appealed to a culture in the midst of an industrial revolution.

3. **Rich should not help the poor**. This is based upon the false belief that the wealthy have somehow earned their fortunes on their own and that they have no social responsibility whatsoever to the less fortunate. The truth is that the capitalist makes his or her fortune in one of two ways; A. exploitation of labor, paying less than the value of work or B. Inheritance; winning the lucky sperm lottery. Helping the poor, they argued, would only serve to delay human evolution by prolonging the existence of the poor. In a society based upon "Survival of the Fittest," helping the poor only serves to obstruct the "Natural Selection" process and human progress.

4. **The poor are encouraged to blame themselves for their poverty**. This is, in many ways, perhaps the most destructive legacy of Social Darwinism as it discourages the impoverished from organizing and demanding justice. It instead encourages them to be ashamed of their condition and ignores the reality of **structural poverty**. Capitalism is structured to create many losers in order that an elite, privileged few may enjoy the luxuries associated with wealth.

"I've seen, firsthand, the kind of shame experienced by the poor," continued Antonelli. "Some years ago, I was a coordinator at an inner city community center. Once a month we would prepare and distribute 'Care Packages'; shopping bags filled with donated groceries and government surplus food products. Surveying the long line of people waiting to get their bag, I could readily see that their body language was protective as they were slumped over and they would never, ever, make eye contact with me, signs of feeling unworthy of even a basic meal. Alas, they were ashamed of their plight and, sadly, did not realize that their condition was by design and not primarily of their doing.

"This deeply held shame of poverty," said Antonelli, "also creates a perverted sense of loyalty to each other as well. I was also the Education Coordinator at the community center and public housing project at the time. I was charged with supervising student attendance from the housing projects to the public schools. I had a gifted young middle school girl, let's call her Amy, blessed with exceptional math and science abilities. I worked tirelessly all summer, gaming the bureaucracy and relentlessly advocating in order to insure Amy a seat at a wonderful math and science magnet school supported by a globally recognized technology university.

"When the first day of school came that September, other students at the project's recreation center informed me that Amy had registered at another, rather poorly regarded, high school. When I confronted Amy and asked her about her decision to pass on an exceptional opportunity, she told me that all of her friends were attending that other school and if she went to the better one she would be considered a geek or nerd and thus be on the outs with her friends. Friends are critically important when you grow up in the projects," Antonelli said. "The poor are too often victims of broken homes and dysfunctional families and your homies are all you've got."

"What became of Amy, I do not know", he continued, "but I'd not be surprised to learn that she now lives in the same public housing project, is perhaps a single mom herself, raising several kids on her own. That's a little glimpse at the beliefs, values and behaviors of the culture of poverty. Anyone who tells you that there is no such thing as a culture of poverty is either ignorant or lying and has most likely never lived in poverty. Remember what we said previously about cultures? That all humans form them. And there are distinctly different cultures for the rich and the poor.

"I know first-hand, since I was the first person in my family to graduate from high school," said Antonelli. "I was a card carrying member of the **Precariat class**, a group of people so poor that negotiating basic survival is indeed precarious, long before I even knew what that term meant We just pretty much lived paycheck-to-paycheck throughout my entire childhood.

"And while some defenders of capitalism might try to say that my 'success' story supports their exploitative system, it's important to note that I survived because of socialist programs implemented by progressives that gave me a fighting chance such as low cost public college tuition, Pell Grants and other forms of federal and state financial assistance as well as Social Security Disability, since my mother was disabled and confined to a wheelchair. If not for the existence of these Democratic Socialist programs, all vehemently opposed by generations of conservative Republicans, I would still be living the subsistence life of a working class ethnic blue collar laborer. I am indeed from 'Poor White Trash.' Were it not for the grace of God and some determined work by people of goodwill with a powerful sense of social justice, I'd still be struggling to survive in the 'hood. Thanks to these programs, I became a first generation high school and college graduate." Antonelli said with some obvious emotion.

"I also endured the reactions of my own friends and family when I became the first to attend college. The snide remarks and bitter resentment of those who viewed me as a kind of traitor to my socio-economic class. My uncle, I remember, one time at a family gathering, shook my hand and animatedly expressed his amazement at how soft my hands were. The product, he loudly announced, of not doing any 'real' work. As a bricklayer," Antonelli recalled, "my uncle's view of legitimate work resulted in calloused and blistered hands. The social situation at university was no better as I certainly didn't fit in with the wealthy or even middle class students and it was often no better when attempting to connect with minority classmates, who often tended, rather understandably, to focus more on race than class.

"What many universities fail to understand is that there's more to diversity than just pigmentation. Many colleges congratulate themselves for recruiting minority faculty, for example, but they often fail to calculate economic class into the equation. They engage in what I call 'Crayola Diversity' where they acquire a box full of different colors but don't understand that they are all still crayons. The beliefs, values and behaviors of middle and upper class culture are fairly consistent regardless of your skin color. This is not to say that people of color do not face unique challenges in our society, but an African –American or Latina professor from the same middle/upper class background as their white male tenured colleague has no more clue or better understanding of the challenges faced by working class students, regardless of color. So, in order to attend college and have any chance of improving my lot in life, I, like so many white working class kids, had to live with one foot in both cultures—home and school—while belonging in neither. True diversity would include recruiting faculty from working class backgrounds. People of any color who were, perhaps, like me, the first in their families (First Generation) to attend college and consequently have personal experience with the unique challenges these students face. We'll talk a bit more about this a little later.

"But never doubt for a minute," Antonelli concluded, "that Social Darwinism has had a deep impact on the fundamental beliefs, values and behaviors of American society, how we are encouraged to view the rich, the poor, the working class and minorities."

Chapter 14

The Gospel of Wealth; Social Darwinism 2.0

"In addition to the promotion of the pseudoscientific rubbish of Social Darwinism," continued Antonelli, "conservative ruling class members, including Robber Barron Andrew Carnegie endorsed *'The Gospel of Wealth'* which was introduced in an essay by Carnegie himself. *The Gospel of Wealth*, published in 1889, essentially accepted most of the tenets of Social Darwinism; that the wealthy were indeed superior, more evolved humans and that vast economic inequality was the 'basic nature of things' and actually good for human progress.

"However, Carnegie did attempt to soften the proposition that the rich should in no way, help or assist the poor. Rather, he proposed that since the rich possessed superior attributes, they should employ them on behalf of the poor. He said it was the **Noble Obligation (Noblesse Oblige, they called it)** of the rich to do so, in ways that they felt appropriate. For example, instead of raising wages and improving working conditions at his plants, Carnegie championed the construction of libraries across the nation; claiming that this would provide the working class with the opportunity to better themselves. Apparently Mr. Carnegie hadn't considered how difficult it might be to take oneself to a library after working a grueling twelve hour day, six days per week in one of his steel plants," Antonelli, sarcastically noted.

"It should come as no surprise, then, to learn that the wealthy quickly adopted Carnegie's approach since it would serve to deter sorely needed government involvement in addressing widespread poverty and subsequently prevent the creation of progressive taxation upon the wealthy classes in order to support such programs.

"This shamelessly patronizing philosophy," he continued, "suggests that the poor are incapable of determining their own needs and further enforces the Social Darwinist view that the rich know best. The takeaway here is this; the rich are NOT special and they did NOT 'work hard' on their own to attain their wealth. In either event it is utterly unconscionable for anyone to possess so much wealth while millions go hungry and homeless. That is precisely the reason that many democratic socialist nations today impose limits on how much money any one person can possess, via progressive marginal wealth taxes, as it presents a threat to democratic processes as clearly evident in the American donor-driven political landscape.

"I also had some direct experience with The Gospel of Wealth's fundamental premise that the rich know best," said Antonelli. "In my job as Education Coordinator in the public housing projects, I had secured a grant from a downtown collaborative of wealthy businesses to fund the creation of an 'Education Resource Center' to be located in the projects. The purpose was to create a safe, quiet, space for children to do homework, assisted by paid tutors. I literally built the center with my own two hands, taking over a long neglected rat and roach infested storage space adjacent to my office at the Community Center.

"I cleared, painted and prepped the room for study," Antonelli recalled, "acquiring surplus desks from the public schools and purchasing lamps, maps and teaching supplies. I was in the process of hiring tutors to assist the kids when we were ready for our Grand Opening. I posted flyers all across the housing project announcing the opening of our shiny new Education Resource Center. And with great anticipation, I purchased donuts and made a vat of coffee on the big night and waited for people to assemble. And waited, and waited.

"You see, the big Grand Opening night finally arrived. And 7:30 became 8:30, became 9:30 and by 11 PM not a single soul had come to check it out. This was a truly teachable moment for me," Antonelli recalled, "since I had used education to escape poverty and held it in the highest regard. Being the kind of kid who used to skip school to go to the library, I would have been thrilled to check out the new center and explore the books on its shelves. But that was obviously not the case here. I had to ask myself why this was so.

"I had often hosted full houses at the community center; rooms bursting at the seams with public housing residents when I brought in members of local trade unions to discuss the process of becoming a plumber, electrician or carpenter. It was then I remembered what it was like attending college without having any direct family who had done so. I was a stranger in a strange land; neither fish nor fowl since I was not truly a part of the college culture nor could I again be fully accepted by my homies. I was stuck with a foot in two worlds, belonging to neither," reflected Antonelli. "The critical difference was that I used to spend my free time, sometimes cutting school, hanging out in Harvard Square surrounded by a world of books and records and people who knew a great deal about both. Knowing stuff was cool there. I wanted to be that kind of cool.

"Like me, the residents of this housing project knew no one who had attended college but unlike me, they couldn't imagine themselves as college students. They had no model for that path but could readily see themselves becoming plumbers, electricians or carpenters by entering a two or three year apprenticeship program. Some of them even knew people who made a very good living doing so.

"*That was it!* I thought. *We had gotten the whole focus wrong!* Instead of emphasizing and prioritizing college as a path out of the projects and poverty, we needed to target vocational education. I immediately arranged for a meeting with the corporate benefactors of my grant to inform them that we would be much more successful if we made vocational education our focal point. I met with them downtown as they would never think of coming out to the housing projects unless accompanied by the media for a photo op. I presented my case to them in a boardroom setting after which I was told that they would take my recommendations under advisement and be in touch.

"Shortly thereafter," continued Antonelli, "I received notice that they had rejected my proposal and would continue funding only a college-centric program. I then submitted my resignation, telling the board that I had escaped poverty myself and, were it not for the grace of God, I might well be a resident of this very kind of project. However, I was not willing to be an enabler for a program which I knew was a demonstrated failure. It would be a betrayal of my social class, I would have had to become a willing collaborator in a ruling class publicity scheme. My soul was not for sale, so, I quit." said Antonelli.

"What's all this got to do with The Gospel of Wealth?" Erin asked.

"Well," Antonelli continued, "the well-heeled capitalist community of that boardroom were products of ruling class/upper middle class families where college was a given, often following their fathers and grandfathers footsteps by attending Ivy League institutions and benefiting from legacy admissions programs. They believed that they knew best what 'those people' in the housing projects needed and were not interested in hearing my first-hand, reality-based, account of why they were mistaken. Textbook Gospel of Wealth stuff; the rich know best, big daddy, patronizing approach to the poor.

"Of course, Social Darwinism and the Gospel of Wealth were and still are both easily and readily employed by racists who, during the Gilded Age, could point to the impoverished and often swarthy complexioned, non-English speaking, new immigrant workers from Italy, Greece, Poland, and the like, and say that their poverty was attributable to the moral flaws and laziness believed by them to be inherent in their ethnic backgrounds. Today the scapegoats are Latinx and Blacks. Same BS, different day. Many of the wealthy Robber Barons, considered themselves to be 'Real Americans,' AKA White Anglo-Saxon Protestants (WASPS) and declared that they had pulled themselves up by their bootstraps, all evidence to the contrary and that the poor masses were simply an inferior breed of human, if human at all. As we have seen, most all wealthy people owe their privileged condition to either the systemic exploitation of workers, inheritance or both. When a wealthyperson tells you that they got rich from hard work and grit, always ask them 'whose?'

"However," continued Antonelli, "a nation built upon the shameful twin pillars of Native American genocide and African American slavery had little difficulty accepting both Social Darwinism and the Gospel of Wealth as a dominant narrative for the American socio-economic landscape and a justification for unimaginable levels of income inequality and unconscionable forms of inhumane brutality.

"While now widely discredited, the barbarously compassionless legacy of both Social Darwinism and the Gospel of Wealth still often emanates from the lips of conservative/Republican political leaders as talking points when they attempt to justify cutting or rejecting government social programs for working and poor people. Often repeating that it is not the government's role but that of private charity to help the poor. The myth of the rich as benevolent dictators, deciding what the poor need and deserve can be readily seen in their repeatedly failed 'Trickle Down' economic policies which rely on the wealthy, with their big tax cuts, to extend benevolence upon workers. Utter absurdity, indeed!" exclaimed Antonelli. "A rudimentary understanding of the elements of predatory capitalism would tell us otherwise. **The objective of capitalism is and always will be to enhance the profits of the capitalist by exploiting labor. Period. End of story.**

"As liberal economist **John Maynard Keynes (1883-1946)** put it: *'Capitalism is the astounding belief that the most wickedest of men will do the most wickedest of things for the greatest good of everyone.'*

"It's long past time that we as a culture admitted to ourselves what we can readily see with our own eyes," said Antonelli, "capitalism does not serve the greater good but only further enriches the elite capitalist class, the 2 percent at the expense of the vast majority, the 98 percent. Predatory Capitalism is, then, an essentially immoral and unjust economic system and no amount of benevolence from our corporatist masters nor charitable initiatives by however well- intentioned religious and social organizations will ever change that simple fact.

"As **Dr. Martin Luther King, Jr**. (1929-1968) said, *'The poor don't need charity; they need justice.'*"

Chapter 15

Democratic Socialism: A Proven Approach

"So what's the solution?!" called out Jamal. "How do 'We the people 'take back our government and economic system to provide for the general welfare of all citizens, not just the wealthy two percent?"

"Ahhh….yes," said Antonelli, chuckling. "There's the rub, eh?

"Well, there's a third way that has not only proven itself in other nations but has, in fact led to the creation of society's that enjoy the highest quality of life for the average citizen according to the United Nations and other international organizations. They include western European nations like Norway, which has been number one in that UN survey for the past seven consecutive years, as well as Denmark (often called 'The Happiest Place on Earth') and Sweden to name but a few.

"They thrive under a political system called **Democratic Socialism**," Antonelli noted.

"Democratic Socialism is, as the name implies, Democratic, in that the people choose their leaders in regularly scheduled elections. This is important to keep in mind because all too often critics of Democratic Socialism, usually Republicans/conservatives will attempt to conflate it with the far more authoritarian system known as Communism. They will make silly statements like, 'Well, if you don't like our capitalist system you can move to Cuba, Russia, or China.' None of which are in fact, Democratic Socialist societies but are actually dictatorships run by and on behalf of a ruling elite—ironically not unlike unregulated, predatory capitalist societies.

"You'll notice that these folks who seek to deceive the ignorant, never suggest that we move to actual, practicing, Democratic Socialist societies like Norway, Denmark or Sweden. Probably because it would indeed, cause some to discover that these nations, while having problems as all societies do, have done a far more effective job of meeting the needs of their people. In fact, true Democratic Socialist societies are amongst the most democratic nations in the world, as democracy is an integral aspect of any true socialist system. Democratic Socialism is nothing more than bringing democracy into the workplace and insuring that everyone has access to the essentials for a quality life- healthcare, housing, education, living wage and pension regardless of their income level or social status. It's a system that uses taxpayer money to benefit all members of a society.

"It's not something anyone need fear," said Antonelli, "although The Right conflates it with communism and vilifies it for their own purposes. However, Democratic Socialism is not some kind of strange foreign conspiracy to undermine freedom and equality. Quite the contrary, Democratic Socialism is the single most successful form of social organization at accomplishing the greatest quality of life for the average citizen and insuring freedom and equality.

"Fact is that Democratic Socialist programs are no stranger to our shores. In his 1944 State of the Union Address, **President Franklin Delano Roosevelt (1882-1945)** introduced the **'Second Bill Of Rights'** which is a textbook example of democratic socialist policies and values."

Antonelli clicked up a powerpoint slide adding, "President Roosevelt said:

'In our day these economic truths have become accepted as self-evident. We have accepted, so to speak, a second Bill of Rights under which a new basis of security and prosperity can be established for all—regardless of station, race, or creed.

Among these are:

- *The right to a useful and re-numerative job in the industries or shops or farms or mines of the nation;*

- *The right to earn enough to provide adequate food and clothing and recreation;*

- *The right of every farmer to raise and sell his products at a return which will give him and his family a decent living;*

- *The right of every businessman, large and small, to trade in an atmosphere of freedom from unfair competition and domination by monopolies at home or abroad;*

- *The right of every family to a decent home;*

- *The right to adequate medical care; and the opportunity to achieve and enjoy good health;*

- *The right to adequate protection from the economic fears of old age, sickness and accident and unemployment*

- *The right to a good education.*

All of these rights spell security. And after this war is won we must be prepared to move forward, in the implementation of these rights, to new goals of human happiness and well-being.

America's own rightful place in the world depends in large part upon how fully these and similar rights have been carried into practice for all our citizens. For unless there is security here at home there cannot be lasting peace in the world.'

"To define it in its simplest terms," continued Antonelli, "**Democratic Socialism is using taxpayer money to collectively benefit society as a whole, regardless of your socio-economic status.** There are many examples of Democratic Socialist programs that have long played an important role in our culture," Antonelli said as he posted a new powerpoint slide:

Some Examples of Democratic Socialist Programs in the United States:

- **Social Security**

- **Medicare**

- **Medicaid**

- **Public Schools**

- **Public Libraries**

- **Public Transit**

- **Roads, Highways and Bridges**

- **Public Parks**

- **Food Stamps (SNAP)**

- **Federal and State Snow Removal**

- **Public Street Lights, Water and Sewer Systems**

- **Public Trash Pickup**

"And that's just a short list," concluded Antonelli, "So rather than the threat to democracy conservative capitalists claim it to be, Democratic Socialism actually insures that equality, opportunity and freedom are enjoyed by everyone. And the fact is that if you have a Social Security number, you're already a card-carrying Democratic Socialist," he said chuckling.

"As **Rosa Luxemburg (1871-1919)** a socialist philosopher and activist, astutely observed, *'There is no democracy without socialism, and no socialism without democracy.'*

"So, more specifically, what is Democratic Socialism?" Antonelli asked no one in particular. "Well, philosophically," he continued, answering his own question, "a Democratic Socialist believes that in a wealthy, moral society, no one should live in poverty. That in order to insure that no one lives in poverty and to close the inequality gap created by capitalism, the government must maintain strong regulations and/or control of five essential sectors."

He then posted the following projector slide:

The Five Pillars of Democratic Socialism:

- **Universal Healthcare**

- **Tuition Free Education**

- **Living Wage/ Universal Basic Income (UBI)**

- **Housing**

- **A Green New Deal**

He then explained each point to the class.

The Five Pillars of Democratic Socialism:

Universal Healthcare

"At some point in their lives, almost everyone will need healthcare. The United States is the only western industrial nation which does not provide its citizens with taxpayer funded healthcare for all. Consequently, medical expenses are the number one cause of bankruptcies in America. Every working American lives with the knowledge that financial ruin can be but one diagnosis away. Think that kind of daily stress doesn't impact overall health?" Antonelli rhetorically asked.

"How did it happen that America, alone amongst western industrial nations, does not provide universal healthcare for its citizens? It started during World War Two (1941-1945) when so many Americans were fighting overseas that there was a labor shortage. Companies had to lure hard to find workers, often women, by offering health insurance as an employee benefit. This employer- provided healthcare continued well after the end of the war in 1945, although a significant percentage of the population already was working at low wage jobs that did not provide health insurance.

"The situation become an outright crisis after 1980 as major US corporations began relocating their manufacturing operations overseas and outsourcing their various business services such as Billing and Human Resources. This process, a deliberate breaking of the social contract between private industry and the community at large, led to millions of displaced workers, who often lost good paying jobs with great benefits in the auto or steel industry for example, and were instead forced to accept work punching a cash register for subsistence wages and no benefits at the local chain convenience store. This is how much of the Midwest went from being the manufacturing capital of the world to the Rustbelt, an industrial ghost town littered with abandoned and rusting factories and plants where workers once made a decent living, took pride in their work and the company's products.

"Unfortunately," Antonelli continued, "President Roosevelt died in 1945, just as World War Two was ending and did not live to implement the major points of his Second (Economic) Bill of Rights which included four of the five pillars of Democratic Socialism; the right to healthcare, education, housing and a living wage. For far too long now private insurance companies and big pharmaceutical firms have been exploiting this medicine-for-money scheme at the expense, suffering, and yes, even unnecessary deaths of millions of working people. In a medicine-for-money system, a cured patient is a lost customer. It's time to end this Ponzi scheme disguised as healthcare and join the rest of the industrially advanced nations by providing universal healthcare for all."

Tuition-Free Education

"As we have previously discussed, public education is ground zero in the battle with the capitalists for the hearts and minds of the working class. In order to best insure that the profiteering corporate education 'reformers' fail to create a generation of mindless cubicle farm animals it's essential that we settle for nothing less than a fully funded, taxpayer supported public school system that creates a safe space for creative teaching as well as exploration and discovery for students. A place where they can develop critical thinking and apply consensus-building skills that will be needed in the newly organized horizontal organizations of a Democratic Socialist economy.

"Lack of funds must not continue to be a barrier to a college education and vocational training. We simply cannot afford to create an entire generation of college graduate debtors who set out into life carrying the immense cost of their education as some kind of ball and chain they must drag with them into the future. Just as publically funded high school education transformed the 20th century, so publically funded state college and vocational education will build a strong societal foundation for the 21st century."

Living Wage

"As we discussed previously," Antonelli continued, "far too many jobs do not pay enough to survive. No one who works a fulltime job should be living below the poverty level. The implementation of a living wage, based on regional cost of living must become the acceptable minimal standard in the new American workplace. Other methods of attaining economic justice for workers include, the right to organize and join labor unions in all fifty states and the elimination of Right-To-Work Laws, as well as organizing cooperatives where all employees share in the profits and have a vote/representation on the board of directors. Yet another approach is floor-ceiling pay formulas in which the highest paid employee can only make 'X' times more than the lowest paid worker. To this end, a $15.00 dollar minimum wage, while not entirely sufficient, provides a good starting point toward the full implementation of a living wage workforce, government as employer of last resort and a universal basic income (UBI). In a moral, modern, society there's simply no reason for poverty to exist. As Indian Independence Movement leader, **Mohandas K. Gandhi** (1869-1948) said, *"Poverty is the worst form of violence."*

Housing

"In a wealthy, moral, first world nation, everyone should have a roof over their head. The epidemic of homelessness, a byproduct of predatory capitalism, is caused by investor speculation. People with money purchasing houses not to live in but to suck life out of with extortion level rents and multiple properties that often remain empty for much of the year only serve to inflate housing prices. The government must take firm control of this essential human need and commit itself to putting a roof over every American's head," Antonelli declared.

"There are any number of ways that this can be accomplished," said Antonelli, "and we should look at some of the approaches employed by successful Democratic Socialist societies such as Denmark, Norway and Sweden. For example, we could build public housing by recruiting people who wish to learn construction trades, thus resolving one problem, a housing shortage, by addressing another, unemployment and re-training. The important thing is that the government, at the direction of the electorate, demand an end to homelessness and set ambitious goals to end the barbarity of entire families on the streets."

A Green New Deal; (GND)

"Modeled after Franklin Roosevelt's historic New Deal, an extensive, multi-faceted economic recovery program of the 1930's, the Green New Deal challenges us to now re-invest in infrastructure, particularly planet friendly energy sources and public transportation which is essential if we are to significantly cut carbon emissions and provide a less costly way for all working people to get to their jobs," said Antonelli. "Alternative energy industries create sustainable power as well as large numbers of desirable employment opportunities. Green industries like solar, wind and biofuel energy are the future and the foundation of any sustainable manufacturing sector. **The unique challenges of the 21st Century require that environmental issues be linked to employment.** The Green New Deal provides an outline, a framework for addressing the urgency of climate change by moving towards a decarbonized economy and eliminating dirty fossil fuels and agricultural emissions while simultaneously creating new good-paying green jobs and providing the essential training to fill them.

"Earlier, we discussed the term Zeitgeist, meaning spirit of the times." Antonelli continued. "The Green New Deal and its admittedly challenging big, bold, ambitious objectives lies in the sweet spot of our 21st Century Zeitgeist. Indeed, should we fail to accomplish many of the GND proposals, there will be no 22nd Century at all. This is not the time for mealy-mouth corporate centrist politicians willing to compromise away the future of the earth itself. It's time to go big or go home. Or rather, lose our planetary home.

"All of this can be accomplished," Antonelli said, "provided we develop a unity of purpose and insist that our government represent the needs of all Americans. **Government priorities must be realigned away from the military-industrial complex and dirty fossil fuels and towards real human and planetary needs.** Needless to say, there must be major changes in the way Washington does business and a new wave of fresh faced elected officials who accept no corporate funds and owe their allegiance <u>only</u> to the electorate must lead this change. This transformation can be markedly expedited by the implementation of term limits for all elected federal government officials. Term limits would also serve to remove more than a few Green New Deal and climate change naysayers, some of which are not only shameless accomplices in planetary destruction but already resorting to such utterly absurd assertions as claiming that the GND will take away our hamburgers, cows and airplane travel.

"The wealthy 2%, who for decades managed to avoid taxes or worst yet have given themselves massive tax breaks must be required to pay their full and fair share. Tax schedules need to be re-written and a minimum 70% marginal tax rate must be placed upon any wealth beyond an agreed upon amount, such as 10 million dollars, as practiced in some other democratic socialist nations. This is hardly a radical or excessive proposal since during the Republican administration of President Eisenhower (1953-1961) the top tax rate was over 90%! Let's be very clear; this tax will **not** be imposed on the 98% working class. It is levied exclusively upon every dollar made **above and beyond** 10 Million dollars income. You can rest assured that more than a few 2% ruling class members and their paid minions will be striving to conflate this into a general tax imposed on everyone- which it is not! This is but only one way in which to fund essential programs such as universal healthcare. Other options include proposals such as a wealth tax of 2% on assets over $50 Million dollars and scaling estate taxes as well as a Wall Street transaction tax.

"We must recognize at some point," continued Antonelli, "that any one person having personal control of vast amounts of money presents a danger to democracy as well as raising serious moral issues. What does it say about a culture that coddles billionaires while tens of thousands go hungry and homeless? We must adopt the Swedish motto of 'A government good enough for everybody.'

"Government and private business should both be run democratically, with workers having a voice in public policy and the company boardroom. The proper focus of a humane, sustainable economy is public need, not private greed. Democratic Socialism seeks to find the 'sweet spot' between corporatist capitalism and authoritarian one-party state communism. **Socialism without capitalism is communism, but capitalism without socialism is fascism.** Democratic Socialism represents a balance between the extremes. It is the single most effective social system and the one which can rightfully point to demonstrable successes in improving the quality of life for the average citizen; as is the case in Norway, Sweden, Denmark and elsewhere.

"Democratic Socialists," Antonelli continued, "while rejecting communist style centrally planned, government controlled economies, believe that workers and consumers who are impacted by industries and financial institutions, like banks, should have a voice in their decision-making process. All stakeholders must have a seat at the table and a voice. This **horizontal rather than vertical kind of business and social organization** takes many forms including worker owned and operated 'Co-Op' industries, profit sharing, and fixed formula Executive -to -Worker pay ratios – models that require that the highest paid employee does not make more than X times as much as the lowest paid worker. **Every Democratic Socialist society must determine for itself what approach and level of regulation is appropriate for them, guided by the principles of the Five Pillars.**

"While Democratic Socialists do not believe that government should have complete centralized control over the economy," Antonelli said, "it is, however, often considered important that certain expensive, essential components be nationalized such as public transit, housing, healthcare and education in order to better create a societal infrastructure that nurtures equality and fosters the development of a more humane, just, and sustainable culture. A few long-established examples of Democratic Socialism in the United States include police and fire departments, public schools and public works departments—all publically funded by tax dollars to protect, educate and provide infrastructure to the benefit of us all. So then, democratic socialism is no stranger to America's shores. It's just that predatory capitalism has managed to strangle the people's will and block the implementation of essential programs as first envisioned by President Franklin D. Roosevelt.

"The present state of affairs where corporations and their small cabal of stockholders determine the fate of people and planet on behalf of their own profits; imposing top-down decisions on workers and destroying delicate ecosystems across the planet, is actually a fairly recent concept and runs in sharp contrast to the ancient tribal values of sharing and caring for one another that characterize most of the long, pre-historic and historic human experience. Democratic Socialism is really a very simple, and re-markably successful approach based on the life-affirming belief that sharing is a basic human quality and the fundamental prem-ise that economic and social decisions should be made by those most directly affected by them. **Democratic Socialist poli-cies are in fact, simply practicing Radical Empathy on a national scale.** This is of course, in sharp contrast to the dark vision of human nature professed by capitalists who believe that people are basically selfish and are only motivated by self- serving purposes such as Adam Smith's 'Invisible Hand'. The concept of humans as individual players in some vicious dog- eat −dog dystopia is actually a relatively recent idea and in sharp contra-diction to thousands of years of cooperative, sharing human ex-perience," Antonelli said.

"Indeed Democratic Socialism's documented successes in nations like Norway, Sweden and Denmark have driven conservatives to blatant attempts to discredit the impressive accomplishments of these countries as well as to conflate the system with that of dicta-torial communist nations such as Cuba, China and the old Soviet Union. This is a long-standing rhetorical practice of The Right, referred to as **'Red Baiting'** as it was commonly employed as a form of intimidation during the Cold War years and especially during the heyday of Republican Senator Joe McCarthy and his life-destroying 'investigations' into 'un-American Activities' during the 1950s.

"Democratic Socialism is successful in a wide variety of societies and each has developed its own unique cultural definition that works for them. Building upon a fairly universal foundation of taxpayer funded, government regulated/owned universal healthcare, public education, living wage, and housing each society has determined how much further government regulation and democratic process must extend in order to best secure the highest quality of life for all its citizens. Some emphasize worker cooperatives where decision making and profits are shared by all workers while others implement maximum and minimum living wages upon private sector firms.

"This is precisely why I opened our discussion today with an explanation of cultures," said Antonelli, "since every nation must decide for itself what their unique cultural definition of democratic socialism will look like. As an American, you might think of it as a logical extension of programs like Social Security, Medicare, Medicaid, and the like. A long awaited fulfillment of President Franklin Roosevelts Second American Bill of (economic) Rights which we discussed earlier." he concluded.

"As **Dr. Martin Luther King, Jr. (1929-1968)** observed,

"We are saying that something is wrong...with capitalism...There must be better distribution of wealth and maybe America must move toward a democratic socialism."

Chapter 16

Attempts to Discredit Democratic Socialism

"The wealthy 2 percent must disparage Democratic Socialism and they do so in a number of ways." began Antonelli

"As we mentioned, the Right employs rhetorical slight- of -hand tactics by suggesting that a Liberal or Democratic Socialist who is not happy with things here should move to Cuba or China. This is, of course, utter rubbish, since neither nation enjoys anything vaguely resembling Democratic Socialism, but it's very effective with the Right's largely ignorant and class-confused followers and often serves as a real show-stopping way of avoiding a serious data-driven debate. A rhetorical tactic akin to the old law school adage that when the law and facts are not on your side you should simply bang on the table.

"With the tearing down of the Berlin Wall and the subsequent demise of the Soviet Union (1989), the capitalist class in the United States needed to find new enemies both external and internal to continue to control the people through fear. 'Radical Islamic Terrorism' got a big boost after the 9/11 attacks (2001) and thereafter, the Right insisted that all immigrants were now to be viewed as potential terrorists including Mexicans, Libyans, and other peoples desperately fleeing from poverty and war. They were all prime candidates for this kind of scapegoating. While a most detestable tactic, one can readily understand why The Right would need to resort to such practices since Conservatives are in the unenviable position of constantly trying to defend an indefensible economic system.

"Because the conservative argument is essentially bereft of intellectual substance," continued Antonelli, "it is essential that they employ a variety of methods to maintain social control and instilling fear plays a major role.

"**Fear** is a very important tool to this end. In fact, fear is the most important tool employed by the ruling class and the driving force used in controlling the masses. Fear of losing ones' job and ending up poor, hungry and homeless is the major motivating force behind keeping the work force docile and subservient. In addition, the daily news is chock full of horrific stories about people who met unspeakably horrible ends in what we are told is a very dangerous world. Add to this the constant threat of terrorism, both domestic and foreign, then include a dash of racist fear of 'the other' and of the poor and one could readily see how people would be frightened. Once adequately frightened, the masses can then be **intimidated** into giving up their rights in the name of national security- literally buying ones safety in exchange for their rights such as surrendering free speech, the right to protest and public assembly since such demonstrations would make a location 'unsafe,' for example. Your government can best protect you, they argue, if you surrender these rights.

"**Distraction** is another crucial element in the social control playbook, and professional sports, celebrity gossip and social media draw the public's attention like a shiny object waved before an infant. This is precisely why protests by professional athletes like Colin Kaepernick are so effective. By taking a knee during the national anthem at football games to protest police brutality against often unarmed blacks, Quarterback Colin Kaepernick interrupted the distractive quality of sports by interjecting a very inconvenient reality of injustice.

"Finally, in order to further underscore the dangerous nature of our society it's useful to employ any number of 'us versus them' wedge issues designed to divide the working class against itself. 'God, Gays, and Guns' as the saying goes, provide an effective array of divide and conquer type issues that keep the working class from uniting and demanding justice from its common nemesis, the ruling capitalist class," said Antonelli. "These faux issues involve religious sectarianism and its dogmas surrounding issues such as abortion and the roles and rights of women; discriminating against the LGBTQ community by denying them adoption and employment rights, military service and economic, social and political equality; and of course the Second Amendment gun control issue all play a part in the divide and conquer ruling class approach to controlling the working class majority. Add to this a healthy dose of fearful racism towards Blacks, Latinx, Muslims, LGBTQ, and anyone else who's different and we have a perfect environment for class confusion and capitalist social control."

Freedom; Two Very Different Definitions

"You may notice that politicians are fond of the term 'Freedom' and use it profusely in their stump speeches," continued Antonelli. "But the word is essentially a feel-good, glittering generality, and has two distinctly different meanings—one for the capitalist and quite another for the worker.

"It's a case of '**Freedom To' vs. 'Freedom From'**. The capitalist class defines it as **freedom to** treat employees as they see fit, pay them what they will and not be 'tethered' by government regulation and taxation. Meanwhile, the working class views it as **freedom from** the ravages of predatory capitalism: including subsistence pay, unemployment, lack of workplace protections, the absence of healthcare, educational opportunities and pensions. It's essential that the working class, the 98 percent, always remember the critical difference in definitions whenever they hear some politician talking about 'Freedom'.

"So, that explains some of the numerous ways by which the capitalist ruling class attempts to divide us and keep us fearful of Democratic Socialism." concluded Antonelli. "Any questions?" he asked but seeing nothing but spinning- wheel minds processing what he'd just said, he continued. "As **President Harry S. Truman (1884-1972)** astutely observed:

'Socialism is a scare word they have hurled at every advance the people have made....Socialism is what they call Social Security...Bank Deposit Insurance....the growth of free and independent labor organizations. Socialism is their name for almost anything that helps all the people.'"

Chapter 17

Wage Slaves and Their Professional Overseers

"So now that we've established some basic terminology and understanding of respective economic theories," said Antonelli, "let's return to my original comment regarding a unified field theory connecting all of this morning's wonderful presentations.

"We were treated to three well researched presentations regarding workers, public education and Earth Day. The single element that ties these issues together and, indeed, creates the problems and challenges within each is Predatory Capitalism.

"The excellent presentation on workers in the Gilded Age took us to the time in which the Robber Barons such as Rockefeller, Carnegie, Morgan, et al, were establishing themselves as America's new ruling class, the 2 percent. Having won the Civil War, the North was now replacing chattel slavery with wage slavery in the factories and mills of New York, Boston, Chicago, Pittsburgh and the like. The assembly lines required tens of thousands of hands working 12 and 16 hour days, six days a week for subsistence wages. Child labor was even cheaper and thus widespread.

It was only banned after a long, hard struggle by Progressives and Labor Union Leaders. Cheap labor being the essential defining aspect of capitalist profiteering, the Robber Barons demonstrated repeatedly that they would go to any lengths, including murder, to maintain control of wages and working conditions. Perhaps no better example of this is the Ludlow Massacre in Ludlow Colorado in 1914 when the Colorado National Guard and guards from the Rockefeller owned Colorado Fuel and Iron Company attacked a tent encampment of strikers and their families, indiscriminately killing men, women and children and lighting their tents on fire, igniting the Colorado Coalfield Wars in which 75 to 200 people were killed. American Historian **Howard Zinn (1922-2010)** has described the Ludlow Massacre as *'the culminating act of perhaps the most violent struggle between corporate power and laboring men in American history.'* (Zinn, H., *The Politics of History: With a New Introduction.* University of Illinois Press, 1990. p.79)

"The long, bloody struggle of organized, union labor is marked by more than a few courageous leaders," said Antonelli, "both women and men, who risked and often lost their lives for opposing the capitalist exploitation of workers. People like **Mary Harris "Mother" Jones, "Big" Bill Haywood, Eugene V. Debs, Samuel Gompers, John L. Lewis, Cesar Chavez and Dolores Huerta** to name but a few. These brave souls challenged not only the capitalists themselves but also the authority and military might of state and federal governments, which were all too often at the beck and call of the industrial ruling class and more than willing to use force to break a strike. Labor's legal right to organize, bargain collectively and when necessary, employ its most powerful weapon, the strike, was itself an arduous struggle and finally attained in 1935 when Franklin D. Roosevelt, our first Democratic Socialist President, signed the National Labor Relations Act, also known as the Wagner Act, into law.

"A strike," continued Antonelli, "is a work stoppage by a labor union in order to financially pressure ownership to bargain in good faith. Stopping production and thus profits has proven to be a very effective bargaining tool for organized labor.

"In the words of union organizer **"Big" Bill Hayward (1869-1928)**, *'The capitalist has no heart, but harpoon him in the pocketbook and you'll draw blood.'*

"However, wage slavery, including child labor, sadly continues unabated today largely in overseas factories including more than a few outsourced American production facilities in nations lacking government regulation and labor laws and/or led by corrupt leaders who can be paid to look the other way by capitalists.

"Today," Antonelli said, "in the United States, the minimum wage is well below the cost of living and creates a permanent underclass of working poor who often hold two and three such jobs only to subsist. This is the cruel reality for minimum wage workers, who are often vilified as lazy or shiftless because they don't improve their condition. Capitalists and their conservative apologists often charge this underclass with an unwillingness to 'pick themselves up by their bootstraps' and improve themselves. While a very effective talking point for Republican politicians and others seeking to divide the working class against itself, the facts tell a very different story as wages earned in these menial, often service- sector jobs cannot keep up with the cost of living. Consequently the working poor may hold two or even three jobs yet remain homeless because they cannot make enough income to put a roof over their heads.

"The MIT Living Wage calculator © is a quick and easy way to end any arguments about 'lazy poor people' since it will swiftly calculate the actual wage necessary to place a workers income above the poverty line in any location in the country. Then you can compare that wage to available jobs in your local newspaper and see the disparity for yourself. (Check it out at: http://livingwage.mit.edu/)

"So then, the struggle for worker's rights and honest pay for honest work did not end with the conclusion of the Gilded Age. In fact, it has only gotten worse as corporations outsource production to lowest bidder nations. It's a race to the bottom for the working class. Marx, of course, would have anticipated this development, since he explained that the capitalist only profits by devaluing (that is exploiting) labor. And consequently, the capitalist will set up shop wherever it's easiest and most profitable to do so.

"One organization that has been uncovering labor abuses at factories and manufacturing plants worldwide is the Institute for Global Labour and Human Rights. (Check out their videos about child labor and worker abuse at https://www.youtube.com/user/nlcnet)

"So we've now seen how capitalism exploits workers and strives to keep them at the subsistence level. **Desperate people make compliant employees and inattentive citizens who can't afford the luxury of demanding justice.** This is the critical role that structural poverty plays in the capitalist model. The very real fear of poverty, due to lack of a comprehensive government-provided social safety net, motivates people to accept low paying menial jobs with deplorable working conditions in order to survive. They are, of course so fearful of displeasing their masters/bosses that they are not involved in political issues that might improve the quality of their lives for fear of losing their marginal jobs. The truth is that the ruling class has no interest in eliminating poverty as it is the prime source of fear and motivation for workers to submit to all manner of detestable conditions and accept the lowest wages. This is precisely why conservatives vehemently oppose any form of government assistance to workers, be it unemployment insurance, Medicaid, or disability insurance, claiming, often in subtly racist 'dog whistle' political speech, that it kills worker's motivation to find employment when in fact it actually forces them to accept subsistence wages and inhumane working conditions," said Antonelli.

The Professional Overseers

"Meanwhile," continued Antonelli, "the middle class earns a more respectable and pleasurable livelihood by serving the professional needs of the ruling corporate elite. Accountants, Lawyers, Doctors, MBA's and the like are all required to service the capitalist class and they are rewarded with "white collar" privileges such as college education for themselves and their children, expendable income, vacations, suburban home ownership and pensions.

"The ethical price of this status is often very high," Antonelli said, "as the professional class must do the bidding of their corporatist masters in terms of disciplining and when necessary firing line workers. They lobby on behalf of a ruling class agenda which includes tax cuts for the wealthy at the expense of programs for the poor, as well as deregulation of their industries at the expense of worker safety, quality of life and environmental justice. They are charged with developing the 'Business Plans,' aka Ponzi Schemes, which most effectively exploit labor –both here and abroad in order to further maximize profits for shareholders. **Any business model that does not include a living wage for workers is nothing more than a nuanced form of slavery.** And no one should work a full time job and bring home an income below the poverty line. That is a fundamental principle of Democratic Socialism.

"This professional class is, themselves, kept in line with both a carrot and stick, class confusion approach. The promise of a corner office and fear of demotion or dismissal keep the professional class in line and on task. This is, sadly, a textbook example of the working class policing themselves, thanks to class confusion via a division of labor; white collar v. blue collar; college v. vocational; skilled v. unskilled. The capitalist class continues its incessant assaults on labor today by opposing living wage initiatives, and proposing legislation that obstructs union organizing and supports 'Right to Work' Laws which undermine unions and keep wages low.

"Capitalists also employ an extensive array of 'wedge issues' designed to divide working people against each other including gender, sexual orientation, and socio-economic background but perhaps none so powerfully as race. The best example of capitalist exploitation of labor is, of course, slavery. While the Union fought a war to eliminate bondage slavery the battle against racism and wage slavery has proven a far more arduous journey," Antonelli said.

"In addition, the ruling class 2% continues to instigate divisions between white and minority workers. Instilling fear and distrust and employing voter suppression and gerrymandering tactics wherever possible. Ironically, the 'Party of Lincoln' can't muster much more than ten percent of the Black vote today as their anti-minority reputation precedes them. This is why landmark legislation such as the **1964 Civil Rights and 1965 Voting Rights Acts**, signed into law by Democratic president Lyndon Johnson, are so important. These laws are designed to protect minorities from both physical and social harm and are intended to defend their right to vote. Unfortunately, the Supreme Court, at the behest of several Republican governed states, recently gutted many of the important oversight provisions in the Voting Rights Act which has led to a marked increase in incidents of minority voter suppression. Since today's Republican base consists largely of older white men, a declining demographic, we can likely expect more gerrymandering (drawing up districts that favor Republican candidates) and voter suppression tactics in the future.

While civil rights laws alone may not change public attitudes, and are often challenged in the courts by Republicans, they represent a major step towards a more democratic future. This kind of legislation is designed to literally outlaw racism until sometime in the future when it is no longer socially acceptable and the ugly and inhumane practice of slavery, a bi-product of capitalism, is but a distant, disturbing memory.

"As civil rights leader **Stokely Carmichael (1941-1998)** said, *'If a white man wants to lynch me, that's his problem. If he has the power to lynch me, that's my problem. Racism gets its power from capitalism. If you're anti-racist, whether you know it or not, you must be anti-capitalist.'*

"Remember this above all else," concluded Antonelli, "**the foundational principle of capitalism is the systemic exploitation of labor.** And history teaches us, time and again, that capitalists will do whatever is deemed necessary, from voter suppression to murder, to maintain their power and control. All of which brings us to the role of education in this capitalist economic landscape."

Chapter 18

Public Education; Battle for Working Class Hearts and Minds

"I started my career as a teacher," began Antonelli, "a high school social studies teacher, who idealistically, sought to educate the next generation of Americans and prepare them to better confront the injustices of the capitalist nation into which they were born. A son of the working class, I was the first in my family to graduate high school. My parents, both blue collar workers, had only middle school educations and scratched and scraped to provide for me and my brother, Ben.

"While there was always food on the table, there was little money for much else. My father, despite his limited formal education, was a reader; a history buff and news junkie who took interest in politics because it directly affected his ability to find construction work. A child of the Great Depression, he idolized Franklin D. Roosevelt and the New Deal, often referring to FDR as 'The father of our country.'

"It was from my dad that I came to fully understand the relationship between politics and prosperity, for we as a family literally survived at times, on government programs such as unemployment insurance and, later, when Mom became physically disabled, I was able to go to state college on Social Security Disability, Pell Grants and other federal and state assistance programs.

"Tuition back then was affordable enough that I could cover it by also working part time during semesters and full time when school was out," recalled Antonelli. "While there was very little margin for error, financially, I was able to keep it together and earn my B.A. in History, Magna Cum Laude by bagging groceries, cleaning public restrooms and painting the interior of factories. It was while performing these menial jobs that I was first introduced to the impact of social class as people would look down on me and bark orders as if I weren't human but rather, a worker from the American 'Untouchable' Caste. However, I also recall that when bagging groceries and carrying them to customer's cars, it was usually the poorest people, of every color, who offered me a tip. A precious lesson about the definition of compassion; 'understanding from suffering', as they fully understood my lowly place on the capitalist food chain and had likely suffered similar degradation themselves. They were practicing the kind of **radical empathy** which we so desperately need amongst the working class, the 98 percent, today.

"It's from those difficult days that I learned to appreciate all who labor on my behalf; to speak kindly with the cashier, grocery bagger, and janitor; to generously tip the table server, knowing full well what those jobs can do to one's sense of self-worth. Like you and me, these people have hopes and dreams, alas aspirations that will be difficult, if not impossible, to fulfill given our present state of late stage capitalism. Unless, of course things change. We, together, make the changes.

"Anyway," he continued, "I wanted to use my position as a teacher to change the brutal economic landscape that I had experienced, to bring my version of radical empathy to the classroom and, hopefully, inspire the next generation. To help educate a generation of socially conscious, politically aware citizens who would go forth and champion economic, social and political justice. People prepared to challenge the status quo and not willing to accept the normalization of systemic exploitation.

"I was very fortunate for much of my thirty odd year teaching career as the capitalists had not yet fully turned their attention to controlling and dismantling the public schools. For the most part, I was the master of my classroom; teaching history from the perspective of the oppressed and developing award winning and extremely popular courses in global studies/world cultures, the 1960's, and philosophy.

"Then, 'No Child Left Behind' happened," Antonelli said. "This was the federal legislation authorized and signed into law by President George W. Bush, in effect from 2002 to 2015, which introduced high stakes standardized testing into the schools. It would become only the tip of the iceberg as increasingly, federal funding to schools was predicated upon increased testing for an ever growing number of subjects and consequently the development of cookbook curriculums for virtually every course.

"I had long wondered exactly how far a capitalist society was willing to go in funding courses which revealed inconvenient truths about capitalism and capitalists; education that could undermine the societal control of the 2%, and I was now about to find out. Turns out, much to my chagrin, that they were not willing to provide the education which might overthrow them," Antonelli said, chuckling.

"The first thing that happened is that the state revoked all of our lifetime teaching certificates and required that we earn 'Professional Development Points' and apply for certification renewals, at our expense, every five years. This was obviously done in order to reign in the more experienced, tenured teachers like myself who were objecting strenuously to the standardized testing- cookbook curriculum plan. Those of us who saw that their objectives had less to do with effective pedagogy than efficient social control could now face loss of our teaching license and livelihood should we decide to object too strenuously to their 'reforms.'

"This, in hindsight, was the moment when teachers unions should have filed formal grievances but, fact is, that all too many teachers unions were not only silent, but complicit.

"And this was, of course, only the beginning of what would become an on-going full frontal assault on public schools. The capitalists now sought to control curriculum in order to produce docile, submissive cubicle farm animals incapable of the critical thinking necessary to challenge their authority. The next generation of labor, as the wealthy 2% saw it, would, ideally, be capitalist bred and raised. What's more, they could even profit from ransacking public school funds. They could literally get paid to implode the public schools and create a new school system more to their liking.

"The capitalist formula was very simple, yet extremely effective," said Antonelli. Striding toward the projector, he posted a slide outlining the corporate hostile takeover of the public schools.

Stages of Corporate Takeover of Public Schools

1. Continuously Embed the Message That Public Schools are Failing (Despite all evidence to the contrary.)

Simply put, public schools, while not perfect, take all comers and the vast majority graduate as literate citizens. The capitalist plan was to make "Failing Schools" the talking point for every bought and paid- for politician, private for-profit testing company, charter school shill, and administrative fop. Shout it from the rooftops, early and often enough and people will believe it. The Big Lie concept writ large.

2. Deprive Public Schools of Funding

Financially deprive public schools of the essential funds to fulfill their responsibilities via budget cuts, and the funding of charter schools. Starve public schools to feed charter schools.

3. Create Tests to Confirm and Verify the False Premise That Schools are Failing.

Enter the for-profit testing companies. Still more siphoning off of desperately needed funds from public schools.

4. Standardize and Privatize the Schools.

Charter Schools, both public and for-profit private charters have been a most valuable tool for undermining the public school and busting teachers unions. They siphon off badly needed taxpayer funds and often the most academically talented students. They then subject their faculty members to de-professionalized color-by-number teaching methodologies while stripping them of union protections regarding working hours, conditions, number of work days, and tenure.

"This overall strategy has been remarkably effective in turning our public schools into test prep centers and creating new markets for profiteering testing companies and union-busting, charter schools. All of which serves to siphon off precious taxpayer dollars to private charter school stockholders who are often free from public accountability." Antonelli said.

"Prior to this corporate assault on public education," Antonelli recalled, "teachers were regarded as classroom professionals wielding much of the authority regarding curriculum and course development. I, myself, created and taught several award-winning and very popular courses in multi-cultural/global education and Philosophy; East and West. This is now, of course, unheard of as teachers are treated like big box store clerks, and handed a cookbook for every course they teach. They are expected to adhere assiduously to that course binder and have no time for reflection and critical thinking skill development with students. In many cases their pay is determined by test score outcomes. **Standardized teaching produces standardized thinking** which is precisely the objective of the capitalist class since this will result in a new generation of submissive, compliant labor.

"Teachers, themselves have been subjected to a systemic de-professionalization of their craft. What we are witnessing is **Taylorism,** which we previously discussed as employed against factory workers, being applied to the teaching profession. And, as on the assembly line, all actions and decisions made by the teacher are pre-approved and serve only the stated 'outcomes' in the curriculum cookbook. In this process, the essential professional responsibilities of teachers to identify individual learning styles and customize curriculum to the unique needs of each student is replaced by a one-size-fits-all curriculum which manages to both bore the gifted student while failing to address the needs of less capable and special needs learners. Asking a professional educator to teach from a cookbook curriculum is like asking Van Gogh to paint via color by number. The product of this corporatist dystopia," continued Antonelli, "would be workers capable of accomplishing the tasks required by their employers but incapable of the critical and creative thinking necessary to revolt or even see their oppressed condition.

"The fundamental, transformative element of the learning experience would be eliminated and the teacher would be held accountable to insure this was so. The Corporate Ed 'Reformers' would see to it that teachers did not address their primary responsibility; to create a learning environment that nourishes and supports critical and creative thinking and a love of learning. As

Brazilian Educator **Paolo Freire (1921-1997)** said, *'What an educator does in teaching is to make it possible for the students to become themselves.'*

"In this capitalist dystopian vision of schools, teachers would be used to produce functionaries, incapable of self-reflection and personal growth," Antonelli said. "It's far easier to control the prisoner when he doesn't realize he's in prison. A working class foot soldier, a card carrying member of the Precariat rolled off the school assembly line, destined to never explore who they are and never question the true causes of their oppression. Making it far easier to normalize the barbaric byproducts of predatory capitalism; poverty, homelessness and abject human suffering.

"This also explains why the conservative agenda often includes vehement opposition to the creation of African-American, Latinx, Women's and LGBTQ Studies as well as labor history. For, as **Freire** observed, *'...without a sense of identity, there can be no struggle...'*

"If you are unaware of your own people's history and struggle it's less likely you will organize to improve the collective lot of the oppressed," noted Antonelli. "If children do not see significant historical figures who look like them, they are led to believe that they are not important and have no impact on the past or present. It's a devastatingly effective form of disempowerment which assists the ruling class 2% in controlling the working class 98%.

"For there is surely as much art as there is science to the teaching craft," said Antonelli. "All professions prepare their practitioners to make professional decisions based on their training and experience; be they doctors, lawyers or psychologists. To deny that professional decision-making authority to the classroom teacher is to de-professionalize and disempower the educator, reducing them to the order-taking level of Taylor's assembly line worker. This education version of Taylorism is seen in efforts to reduce/stagnate pay and benefits as well as remove tenure for teachers. Further serving to make teaching a less desirable option for talented young people considering a career-the kind of person who just might object to their working conditions. The elimination of tenure prevents the educator from **speaking truth to power** on behalf of students and staff and makes the faculty as a whole more compliant to the capitalist agenda."

"The teacher, at days end," continued Antonelli, "is the only long term stake holder in our schools. While administrators move on to promotions in other districts and parents lose interest as their children graduate, it's the classroom educator who must regain the moral and professional authority as spokesperson for the best interests of students. **Teaching is essentially a healing profession.** Teachers are midwifes of learning and assist students in the transformational journey of becoming more fully actualized human beings. Their voice must be heard and, once again respected.

"Teachers Unions, while all too often complicit in this corporate 'reform' process, have also been disempowered, by non-educators from the business community such as Billionaires Bill Gates (Microsoft Founder & CEO) and Betsy Devos (U.S. Secretary of Education), They have used their fortunes to purchase the public megaphone and wrest authority rightly reserved for professional educators," Antonelli noted.

"The struggle for control of our public schools and restoration of teacher professionalization is Ground Zero in the battle against corporate determination of what the next generation of workers will know and whether they will possess the essential critical and creative thinking skills to challenge the capitalist agenda," said Antonelli. "The result of standardized, one-size-fits-all education is an individual bereft of historical context, inexperienced at critical and creative thinking, and incapable of even discerning their own oppression. Indeed, they lack the essential love of learning as well as the curiosity fundamental to exploration and discovery which may serve to improve their condition.

"Teaching is, historically, the most noble and highly regarded profession and few civilizations have prospered by degrading and disrespecting those who teach. **Alexander the Great (356-323 BC)**, a famous leader and military man of the ancient world, was once asked who he was most grateful to; his biological parents or his teacher, the great philosopher, **Aristotle (384-322 BC).** *'To my teacher,'* he replied, *'I am indebted to my parents for living but to my teacher for living well.'*

"Few indeed, are the civilizations which prospered without honoring the teaching profession and acknowledging its importance to their collective advancement." said Antonelli. "The Chinese proverb on Ms. Kaufman's coffee mug is an excellent example; 'A teacher for a day is like a parent for a lifetime.' Pretty much says it all. There is a certain immortality inherent in teaching as ones students continue to remember and advance what they have learned from you, passing it along to the next generation. In order to preserve this most sacred passing of the torch of knowledge from one generation to the next we must liberate teachers from color-by-number pedagogy and cookbook curricula so that they may, once again inspire critical and creative thinking in our young people; so they may, in Alexander the Great's words, teach students how to live well. Teachers are, in fact, preservers of civilization. They are the ones who help create a society worthy of defending. They are the civilizers of civilization, and consequently, in a moral society, should receive a military style retirement after twenty years of distinguished service. **One of the most destructive effects of capitalism is that it quantifies and commodifies everything.** It views everything as a commodity, a product to be bought and sold to a customer. We as educators must make it emphatically clear that education is not a commodity or product. Students are not customers. Teachers are not assembly line workers and schools are not factories. Teachers unions must become more vocal in this regard.

"You know, in my thirty plus years as an educator, I have had the honor and privilege to help shape and develop the conscience of two generations. There have been many memorable students and classroom moments but none so personally important to me as the day I had completed a class I was teaching at a local college and was walking down the corridor, briefcase in hand, when I was hailed by one of my students, a non-traditional (older) student, an African American women who was wiping away tears with a Kleenex, and said 'I've never heard a white person talk like that.'

"I was deeply moved by her emotional and heartfelt words," Antonelli recalled, "but, let's keep in mind that all I had done in class was speak the truth about the history and present condition of blacks in this country since slavery. I spoke about Black Codes, Jim Crow, 'Separate but Equal,' Brown v. Board of Education, Loving v. Virginia, the killing of Trayvon Martin, and the seemingly countless incidents of police shooting unarmed black men, in some cases children, and virtually never being held accountable and brought to justice. The events that led to the creation of Black Lives Matter. I spoke of the courageous conduct of then NFL Quarterback Colin Kaepernick, who took a knee for justice during the national anthem in protest of police brutality against the Black community. In short, I was using my status as a tenured teacher for its true purpose; **to speak truth to power.** And that is precisely why the capitalists want to eliminate tenure as part of their comprehensive program for hijacking public education and requiring teaching and curriculum that serves their agenda.

"Teachers and their unions must become a loud and persistent voice defending the teachers' professional classroom decision making authority; rejecting cook book curricula and uniform outcomes. Students must not be viewed as so many tires coming off an assembly line. Teachers unions must call out and denounce Draconian budget cuts and explain to the general public that **the teacher's working conditions are a students' learning conditions. Standardized teaching produces standardized thinking.** It disempowers both teacher and student and extinguishes the vital flame of curiosity essential to the development of life-long learners. And while creating a generation of docile, disinterested and compliant cubicle farm animals may serve the interests of the capitalist 2% and their insatiable desire to exploit labor, it does not serve the best interests of students and most certainly violates the moral and ethical standards of the teaching profession.

"Indeed, the entire concept of the school must be transformed in order that it may better reflect values and practices that support horizontal organization and self- government," said Antonelli. "The school should represent our highest aspirations and not simply model top-down hierarchical capitalist subservience. Experiments with teacher-student run schools should be encouraged, where classroom teachers serve as principals on a rotating basis and students have a voice and a vote in the decision-making process. **Schools must be a place where the essential skills of consensus seeking and inclusive decision–making are practiced in preparation for citizenship in the new more democratic economic landscape.** A place where all workers share in the fruit of their labor and have a voice in their company's decision making process. These are the characteristics which best reflect education for democracy rather than autocracy.

"Schools need to be transformed into comprehensive community centers which do not close down at 3PM but instead become the location of adult education and public health and recreation programs. ESL, Citizenship courses and continuing education programs should become the focus of the public school's 'Night Shift' and publically funded re-training opportunities should be available there as well as medical services.

"In such settings, both students and teachers live and practice the skills of democratic governance while developing and encouraging critical and creative thinking as life-long learners," concluded Antonelli.

"As the great Irish poet **William Butler Yeats (1865-1935)** said, *'Education is not the filling of a pail but the lighting of a fire.'*

"And if you remember nothing else, remember this," Antonelli said assertively, **"Everyone considers themselves an education expert because they were once a student. Unless you've actually taught in a public school; unless you've literally had chalk dust under your fingernails, you are no more an authority on education than you are a master mechanic because you've started a car."**

(Author's Note: For more on the cultural importance of teachers, see my column "Thank a Teacher for Their Service" at https://dancamilli.com/firstblog/thank-a-teacher-for-their-service/).

Chapter 19

Diversity: A More Inclusive Approach to Inclusivity

Just then, Jamal shouted out a question. "Ms. K. told us that you also attended Harvard. Is that true?"

Antonelli chuckled and said, "Yes, I admit to having a graduate degree from Harvard. Guilty as charged," he kidded. "However, I can damn well assure you that my parents didn't donate a million dollars or so to build a new boathouse or shiny dorm building. I was definitely not a Legacy Applicant. And, unlike some well-to-do applicants to elite universities, my parents certainly didn't have cash to pay someone to take my admissions exam or write my application essay. I am the ruling classes' worst nightmare; a working class kid with a ruling class education who refuses to forget where he came from. I learned much from my time at Harvard, long the finishing school for the sons of the ruling class. As a 'Townie' or local working class person, attending Harvard provided me with the rare opportunity to experience first- hand, the world of the 'Gownies' or Harvard students who don gowns and parade through Harvard Square on Commencement Day each year.

"In more recent years, Harvard has tried to address some of the institutional inequities inherent in such an archetypal pillar of white Anglo-Saxon ruling class privilege and admit more qualified working class whites like me as well as minority and female students which is all well and good. However, their version of 'Diversity,' like that of many institutions, is flawed since it tends to focus almost exclusively on race and largely fails to address socio-economic class.

"Frankly, there's not much difference between a black or Latino professor who comes from an upper middle class or better background and the tenured white guy in the next office. They share many values based on their economic status. Despite their best intentions, neither can truly understand the day-to-day struggles of working class and poor people and our utter bewilderment when air dropped into the ruling and professional class world. It's what I call **'Crayola Box Diversity'** because when you look in the box, there appears to be a great deal of diversity- so many different colors. But when you empty the box, upon further examination, you realize that although they may be very different colors, they are all still crayons. All essentially the same. And, unfortunately this is also true of many people from racially diverse backgrounds who hail from the same socio-economic class.

"As a working class kid, whose family crest bore the crossed pick and shovel," continued Antonelli, "there was no one there to effectively mentor or advocate for me. No one from an ethnic, working class background on the faculty, perhaps a first generation college grad, who had intimate, personal experience with working class culture and could help me navigate my way through the beliefs, values and behaviors of mainstream Harvard culture. I and my fellow working class comrades were essentially cast adrift to fend for ourselves. Or as Harvard calls it, 'Every tub on its own bottom.' I would hasten to note that some tubs are considerably larger and sturdier than others and students with professional parents, perhaps a legacy admission or two in the family album, were entering a world with which they were intimately familiar and had long ago acquired the skills to navigate effectively. It's important to note that the ruling class 2% have long used elite universities as finishing schools for their offspring. They've essentially weaponized the very term 'education' into a euphemism for socio-economic class. So, if Harvard and other institutions of higher learning are serious about developing a truly diverse learning environment they must recruit professors from actual working class backgrounds, who, like myself, were the first to graduate high school- never mind college. Then have them mentor students like me through the gauntlet that is Harvard culture.

"There's an important difference between diversity and inclusion," continued Antonelli. "Many institutions, however well intended, have defined diversity exclusively by color, gender and sexual orientation and that rather myopic view leaves many economically oppressed people, like me, out of the process. We need to see more inclusion as well as diversity. **Diversity means that everyone gets invited to the ball, but inclusion means that everyone gets to dance.** We must learn to respect the experience and suffering of all working class people regardless of their historically and socially constructed position in the capitalist's food chain. And yes, that must include ethnic working class people. True inclusion means that no one, including ethnic working class people, is marginalized. You might consider this problem somewhat akin to the feelings of many working class women who have, justifiably, felt excluded from the feminist movement. This has, thankfully, begun to be addressed by the inclusive nature of organizations like today's #metoo Movement. And most recently, institutions like Harvard have begun 'First Generation' programs which will, hopefully begin to directly address the inclusion process. Dr. King's comments about judging people by the content of their character and not the color of their skin must be applicable to everyone.

"So then, if English Physicist **Stephen Hawking (1942-2018)** is correct when he says**, *'Intelligence is the ability to adapt, to change.'*** I guess we'll find out just how intelligent places like Harvard actually are." concluded Antonelli, with a wink.

"So then, enough about my Harvard experience. The same kind of alienation is experienced by working class people in the professional world which is why some businesses offer courses in formal table etiquette and decorum as part of executive/professional training. A working class professional, regardless of how skilled and knowledgeable, has no personal experience with the beliefs, values and behaviors of professional culture. To many of us, a network is a television station. Not knowing the code can be very costly. It can cost you a promotion or even your job. Which is why I always encourage my working class students to watch carefully, learn the code, gain tenure, the practice partnership or the corner office and share the rules with your working class colleagues through mentorship. By so doing, we can work to transform the culture from the inside. Just never forget where you came from. That's radical empathy in the workplace,"Antonelli, said.

"Where were we? Oh, yeah, education. So the battle for control of public education is critical to the advancement of the entire working class, the 98%. Only a well-educated, critically thinking citizen can address and resolve the social, economic and political injustices endemic to our capitalist society and work to change them. And that's precisely why the ruling class 2% is hell bent on preventing this from happening in our schools," he concluded. "This is the reason that taxpayer-supported tuition free college and vocational education is one of the five fundamental pillars of Democratic Socialism."

Chapter 20

Capitalism and Environmental Justice

"Which brings me, at last," said Antonelli, "to the devastating impact of capitalism on our planet. In addition to the systemic exploitation of labor, capitalism profits at the expense of the Earth. The degradation of air, water and soil quality as well as the now increasingly frequent occurrence of earthquakes due to fracking, are all attributable to a panoply of capitalist industries extracting resources and/or dumping debris onto Mother Earth.

"As Reeya and Fiorella so eloquently pointed out, the first Earth Day was prompted by a huge oil spill off the coast of California, despoiling miles of pristine beaches and doing untold damage to delicate ecosystems. Consequently, public awareness and environmental consciousness was expanded throughout the United States and the world."

"I'm old enough to remember the bad old days going to public school in Boston," Antonelli said. "My walk to and from school required the crossing of a bridge over the historic Charles River. Alongside that river was a dry cleaning plant that emitted raw, untreated, toxic waste materials through an open drainpipe directly into the river. Back then we were too young and ignorant to realize what an unspeakable environmental crime we were witnessing but instead, used to marvel at how often the color of the river would change as the plant dumped deep reds, neon orange and florescent green chemicals into the water. Frightening just to remember those days, as the river would be one color on the way to school and another upon our return.

"Earth Day marked a dramatic change from the days of environmental ignorance and began the process of public activism pressuring government to end such destructive environmental practices. The public pressure for action was so intense that it was a Republican President, Richard Nixon who signed a bill creating the Environmental Protection Agency in 1970. Ironically, Republicans have often threatened to close down or attempted to severely curtail the agency and its mission ever since.

"Even still more ironic," continued Antonelli, "it was Republican Teddy Roosevelt, the first Progressive occupant of the White House, often called 'the conservation president' who, against strong opposition from members of his own party, doubled the number of National Parks and enacted the antiquities act of 1906, which empowered him and future presidents to set aside federal lands of historic and scientific significance as National Monuments.

"Do keep in mind that Teddy Roosevelt was a pre-1965 Republican and like many other members of his party then, he was an unabashed progressive and social reformer. Ever notice that today's GOP hardly ever mentions old 'TR?'" Antonelli asked. "That's because the Republican Party has moved very far right of many of Teddy's policies and programs. For example, have you ever heard of a Republican today, who believes in setting aside huge tracts of federal land for the exclusive purpose of public recreation and enjoyment, not to be disturbed by corporate mining, lumbering, or other such mineral extraction or business activities? How about finding me a present day Republican who breaks up corporate monopolies and defends the rights of workers to organize into unions and collectively bargain?" The class responded with incredulous laughter to which Antonelli added, "yeah, good luck with that, right?

"Sadly, today's Republican Party has mostly lived up to its reputation as 'the handmaidens of the boardroom' as their policy agenda almost exclusively serves the wealthy 2% which Teddy boldly challenged in his day. In our age of the Citizens United Supreme Court decision, which permits corporate money to impact elections, the Republican Party has pretty much climbed completely into bed with the wealthy corporate capitalist class, the 2%. And the temptation of campaign cash has lured far too many Democrats into climbing into bed with fat cats as well. Perhaps the difference, such as it is, would be that while many Democrats have slipped under the sheets with oligarchs, some have managed to at least keep one foot on the floor. That is to say, the Democrats have payed, at least token attention to the needs and desires of the 98% working class, but none the less have drifted far afield from the policies of FDR and LBJ. Far too many establishment Democrats have almost as little appetite for a new edition of LBJ's 'War on Poverty' as do Wall Street Republicans. And that leaves the working class without a strong voice in either of the two major parties,"Antonelli said, shrugging his shoulders.

"This, of course, creates a daunting political landscape for real progressives and democratic socialists who wish to truly represent the interests of all Americans and provide them with a voice in both government and business. The greatest threats to our planets' delicate eco-systems today are very much the same perpetrators as in both of the Roosevelt's day; corporate capitalists, the 2%, and their insatiable quest for greater profits. Growth at all costs is their mantra. And the only altar they bow before is that of the shareholder and the quarterly statement. Complete exploitation of people and planet is the business plan and un-regulated growth is the Holy Grail. Sustainability be damned. Their bottom line is the bottom line. This is, of course a pathway to self- destruction. As American environmental writer, **Edward Abbey (1927-1989)** noted, *'Growth for the sake of growth is the ideology of the cancer cell.'* "

Chapter 21

Radical Empathy; Capitalism is an Un-Natural Act

"In many ways," began Antonelli, "the environmental movement began in earnest with that first Earth Day in 1970. Built, of course, upon the solid foundation of Rachel Carson's epic work, 'Silent Spring'. However, I remember the early celebrations as being something of a hippie holiday with thousands of sandal clad, pot smoking college age people gathering in public parks and on university campuses across the nation. Few, it then seemed, could have imagined that Earth Day would, one day become a multi-generational, global celebration of and re-commitment to protecting our planet. That fact alone, is tribute to our ability, as a species, to adapt and grow. Let's hope we do so fast enough to save ourselves and the other species with whom we share this, our planetary home.

"That's the amazing thing about public consciousness," Antonelli observed. "It doesn't necessarily require a majority, just a **critical mass**. It happens when we start to think beyond ourselves as individuals and become more fully aware of our essential connectedness to all other people, living things and to the planet itself. This always reminds me of how, as a young student of Buddhism, when my thinking or behavior was overly isolated and self-centered, my teacher would simply raise his hand and wiggle his fingers–thus pointing out that they all appear to be individual but by looking deeper, we discover that they are, in reality, all connected. It's that kind of deeper reality that we tap into when developing social consciousness. Because we are, indeed, all connected, **sharing is a natural human behavior** – that's why it feels so good to help others and contribute to the common good. It's a practice I refer to as **Radical Empathy**. **And Democratic Socialism is Radical Empathy writ large.** Selfishness, contrary to what many conservatives would have you believe, is un-natural and is actually a learned behavior, encouraged by the predatory capitalist Dominant Narrative into which we were all born.

"As a learned cultural behavior," observed Antonelli, "greed and selfishness can also be unlearned provided the fear of scarcity and competition are replaced by that of sharing and cooperation. The capitalist, by necessity, willfully and immodestly ignores the fact that the same size hole in the earth awaits us all. That's precisely why conservatives emphasize competition and encourage us to be afraid. Afraid of the 'Other', afraid of the stranger, afraid of each other. The fear of unemployment and poverty serve a functional purpose for the capitalist. They force people to take unpleasant jobs and be submissive employees. The 2 percent have little reason or motivation to eradicate poverty and homelessness. It' serves an invaluable purpose as a daily reminder to the working class to toe the line- or this could be your fate.

"However, a critical mass of enlightened individuals can change the entire repressive dynamic," said Antonelli. "If you consider the sea change we've witnessed in say, public attitudes toward women's rights in but a few short years you can readily see that a focused, determined group, such as the #metoo movement can indeed shift the beliefs, values and behaviors of a culture—especially in this age of social media. This is why conservatives often oppose net neutrality and prefer a pay-class service structure in which the more you pay, the faster and more extensive is your internet. The cyber network is the global public square of the twenty-first century, a place where people around the world can instantaneously express their views and share information. It can be used as a powerful organizing and educational tool to mobilize global action against the capitalist establishment. Don't ever doubt that this is precisely why they seek to place price restrictions on its usage; just as they seek to control our public school curricula.

"Another example of a major shift in social consciousness would be that of recycling," Antonelli continued. "Back in the '70's recycling was looked upon suspiciously by some as a kind of hippie, socialist plot to undermine capitalist consumerism, which, ironically, on another level, it is! Today, however, you will see recycling bins strewn along curbsides in even the most conservative, Republican neighborhoods. What changed? Public attitudes did. How? Originally, a small number of activists began an education and advocacy campaign; going door to door and explaining the importance of recycling; speaking at town hall gatherings and school committee meetings, actively encouraging recycling and explaining the sustainability concept to the public at large. And today, recycling is a common practice in virtually every city and town across America. All thanks to a small group of committed individuals seeking to make the world a better place. As renowned American Cultural Anthropologist and signatory of the Earth Day Declaration described by Reeya and Fiorella, **Margaret Mead (1901-1978)** observed, *'Never doubt that a small group of thoughtful, committed citizens can change the world; indeed, it's the only thing that ever has.'*

"And all of this bodes very well for our efforts at creating a more humane, sustainable society and ultimately, planet through the implementation of democratic socialist principles," concluded Antonelli. "Providing working people with a voice in both government and business, and insuring that everyone justly share in the fruits of their own labor. The lessons learned from public transformation on issues such as women's rights, recycling and most importantly, Earth Day provide us with inspiration and methods for creating deep, meaningful social change."

Chapter 22
The Struggle for Justice

"The underlying, connective thread which impairs and obstructs progress in all of the societal issues presented by the class today," Antonelli said, "be it labor, education or environmental justice is an exploitative, immoral, and unsustainable economic system called **Predatory Capitalism.** It has made us accept the unacceptable as normal; homelessness, poverty, lack of healthcare and educational opportunities, and the systemic destruction of the fragile ecosystems of planet earth. **The problem with capitalism is that, eventually, you run out of people and planet to exploit.** That day is fast dawning. But *'power concedes nothing without a demand'* as African-American abolitionist **Frederick Douglass (1818-1895)** said, and that's precisely why politics is so important.

"We working people from all walks of life, every background, gender and sexual orientation, must commit ourselves to speak truth to power and demand economic, social and political justice for everyone—including the planet, itself. **We speak for all of Earth** and can no longer abide a system that provides so much for so few at the expense of so many. You may be asking yourself why you should make the sacrifice of time and energy to work for justice when you may well not realize any of the rewards for your efforts during your lifetime.

"Well," he continued, "the struggle for justice is much like the building of the medieval cathedrals in Europe. Many cathedrals took over a century to construct, with multiple generations of craftsman involved in the work. Knowing full well that they would not live to see the fully completed structure, each generation, nonetheless, had the faith that their contribution would lead, one day, to their children or children's children actually experiencing the completed project. The struggle towards justice is much the same, as each generation benefits from the work of the previous one and we presently stand on the shoulders of giants who suffered and struggled to get us to this point. We have a solemn responsibility to honor their memory by doing all we can on behalf of advancing justice before passing the torch to the next generation.

"As American theologian and social ethicist, **Reinhold Niebuhr (1892-1971)** said, **'Nothing that is worth doing can be achieved in our lifetime.'**

"The willingness to take action on behalf of a better future you're unlikely to see is, indeed a characteristic of a great culture. It's a powerful act of **radical empathy**. There's a Greek proverb, *'A society grows when old men plant trees whose shade they know they shall never sit in'*

"So then," continued Antonelli, "while we do, indeed, benefit from the struggle of previous generations who fought so that children might attend public schools rather than work, women might vote and workers might have unions, we also have an obligation to carry the torch forward and earnestly engage in the struggle for justice in our own time. And this struggle continues on behalf of labor, education, people and planet. What we've done here today is practice **authentic history** which, unlike the rote memorization too often presented in our schools, attempts to **connect the dots** between events and respective struggles in order to see the deeper, underlying, more powerful forces at work toward maintaining an unjust system on behalf of a privileged few. It is only through the lens of authentic history that we can identify and root out the fundamentally unjust forces that serve to oppress working people of every color, creed, gender and background. **Authentic History examines power relationships and helps better identify and understand social, economic and political hierarchies of oppression, be they based on race, gender, sexual orientation or class.**

"Anyway," concluded Antonelli, "that hopefully, explains the negative impact of the 'Unified Field' of predatory capitalism upon todays' student presentations about workers, education and the environment. It also demonstrates the ways by which we can more readily identify the real obstacles to justice and transform our collective consciousness to more humane, sustainable perspectives through practicing radical empathy."

"The evils of capitalism are as real as the evils of militarism and evils of racism."

Dr. Martin Luther King, Jr. (1929-1968)

Chapter 23

The Challenges Ahead

"The difficulty lies not so much in developing new ideas as in escaping from old ones" **John Maynard Keynes, British Economist (1883-1946)**

"**N**ow that we have correctly diagnosed the disease to be predatory capitalism," began Antonelli, "and we are no longer confusing the underlying cancer of capitalism with its symptoms such as racism, sexism, poverty, and the despoliation of the earth, we can better understand the breadth and scope of the task before us. **The first order of business is that we must rid ourselves of the deeply embedded cultural misperception, the capitalist dominant narrative, which defines the productive value of a human being as their intrinsic worth.**"

"Those of us who have now awakened from our long class confused slumber and can no longer accept widespread poverty, hunger, homelessness, lack of health care, poor quality public education, racism, sexism, homophobia and planetary destruction as 'normal', must now come together as one voice to demand an end to this unspeakably barbaric capitalist system and the creation of new, more democratic social structures."

"As **Dr. Martin Luther King Jr.** (1929-1968) observed, *'The problems of racial injustice and economic injustice cannot be solved without a radical redistribution of political and economic power.'*

"We must then, implement democracy in **<u>both</u>** our government and business organizations," said Antonelli. "Workers must be empowered with a voice in the workplace as well as a fair share of the fruit of their labor. In order to do this we may look for ideas and inspiration from any number of democratic socialist nations including Norway, Sweden and Denmark. **Every culture interprets Democratic Socialism in its own unique way but the underlying, foundational principles remain the same; in a moral society, no one should live in poverty and democratic, public control/regulation of healthcare, education, living wage, and affordable housing, are essential for anyone to lead a life of dignity.**

"In order to accomplish this, we must change our long -standing conception and practice of hierarchical 'top-down' organizations and transform them into more **horizontal 'consensus driven' organizations** in which all stakeholders are heard, respected and paid fairly for their labor. Profit- sharing must become the new business norm as well as the implementation of top – to- bottom pay scale ratios which insure that the highest paid employee receives no more than 'X' times as much as the lowest paid worker and everyone receives a **living wage**–that is a wage above the poverty level.

"We must restructure our business schools," continued Antonelli, "and design curriculum that prioritizes **production for human need, not greed**; and provides **equitable sharing of profits** by all employees. The cooperative, profit-sharing model must become the standard organization of any acceptable business plan.

We must stop teaching that profiteering on another's labor is a 'shrewd' business plan. To this end, **Democratic Socialism is a moral idea as well as an economic one**.

"While this will serve as a sound foundation for a humane, sustainable society, we must also address several other unique challenges before us as we move into the 21st Century and confront the dangerous death throes of late stage capitalism."

Again, striding towards the projector, Antonelli posted this slide and guided the class through it:

Some Unique Twenty-First Century Challenges:

Automation

A primary cause of worker displacement in the 21st century, automation must be managed in a fair and equitable fashion. Automation and Capitalism are dangerously interrelated. Automation presents capitalists with an opportunity for which they have long aspired; to make poor people and many workers literally useless. We must, as a culture, beware of **techno-chauvinism** and **techno-centrism**, **which advances the idea that technological solutions are superior to all others.** That is why Democratic Socialism requires that ALL stakeholders have a voice in the decision-making process. This better insures that technological advances are applied humanely and not exclusively for the elimination of labor.

"When was the last time that a new technology was implemented for the actual benefit of workers?" asked Antonelli. "I won't hold my breath waiting for your reply," he chuckled.

"Automation makes it much easier for the ruling class to destroy our hard won yet woefully inadequate social safety nets such as Social Security, Medicare, Medicaid, and Unemployment Insurance. **It is critical then, that we not permit the dark,**

profit-driven vision of the 2% to be realized but instead use automation as an opportunity to move further away from traditional roles in the master-slave employment arrangement.

"For example," Antonelli continued, "what will become of the forty-five year old truck driver displaced by self-driving autonomous vehicles? Within the next few short years we will see the introduction of the driverless vehicle which will displace tens of thousands of truckers virtually overnight. We must provide them with both living wage compensation and training to re-enter the workforce in other more sustainable industries, ideally the fast-growing green industries essential to both economic and planetary well-being.

"To this end we must, ultimately, establish **Universal Basic Income (UBI)** presently being tested in places like Stockton, California, Ontario, Canada, and Finland. **Universal Basic Income ensures that all citizens receive income greater than the established poverty level, whether they work or not.** This may also include using the government as an employer of last resort. Many other cities and countries around the world are also experimenting with this approach, which will undoubtedly be necessary in the age of automation- driven worker displacement as well as an essential component of the new, post-capitalist society. We must learn all that we can from the locales experimenting with this approach which includes Utrecht, Netherlands, Namibia, and the longest running UBI program located in Nairobi, Kenya. And for those critics who claim such a program will not work in a larger, more populated nation such as ours, I point to China, which is now also experimenting with their own form of Universal Basic Income.

"No longer will the threat of wage slavery hold workers hostage to the demands of capitalists thus freeing every individual to better fulfill their greatest human potential. This represents a major paradigm shift away from the customary focus on employment as many people will simply not be able to find any work. We must as a society, acknowledge their intrinsic worth as human beings," said Antonelli, "finally discarding the capitalist measure of productivity in determining the value of people, and provide for everyone's basic needs including healthcare, education, housing, and basic income necessary to lead a dignified existence. Failure to treat the expanding numbers of automation- displaced people in this humane manner will only lead to an ever worse kind of capitalist dystopia, an ugly and even more barbaric extension of our present bleak economic landscape. A nation where a very elite few live in luxury while the masses subsist in hopeless squalor, and the ever-expanding **Precariat** live on the precarious fringe of survival. How we treat the growing numbers of 'unproductive' and 'unemployable' people will say much about us as a society and a species."

The Homeless Crisis

"As previously mentioned, providing homes for the homeless can be readily transformed into an opportunity to teach useful building trade skills to workers constructing housing based on need, not greed. Greater government regulations must be placed upon housing and we must affirm that **having a roof over one's head is not a privilege but a basic human right**. In the coming humane, sustainable society, no one should be speculating and profiting from such a critical and essential human need. We must end the commodification of housing. The basic operating principle should be that no one gets a second house until everyone has a home." Antonelli said.

"The homeless crisis was made much worse in 1980 by Republican President Ronald Reagan's 'deinstitutionalization' of the mentally ill who had previously lived in community centers and half way houses. These people were often incapable of caring for themselves without assistance and ended up living on the streets. My brother, Ben, was one of these people," said Antonelli, sadly. "I'll talk more about him later, however we have a self-created housing shortage as capitalism has yet again commodified a basic human need and essentially priced out large segments of the working class population, whether they suffer from mental illness or not.

"Because of my brother's experience, I guess I have a special sensitivity when confronted by a homeless person. I will sometimes duck into a convenience store and buy them a sandwich and a bottle of water and I often carry around a 'Homeless Care Package' which is a plastic bag containing some granola bars, fresh socks and five bucks to hand out. Sometimes I think the reason I continue to stay active in the anti-homelessness movement is that I'm damned tired of handing out sandwiches," Antonelli said, with a somewhat sardonic chuckle. "Here's an idea," he continued. "How's about we provide jobs for the unemployed constructing affordable 'Green' housing? We can be teaching them marketable building trade skills while getting the homeless off our streets. Win-Win, no?! Kinda solves two problems at the same time, now doesn't it?" he said.

Healthcare for all

"Needless to say, universal, government regulated, tax-payer funded healthcare must also become the law of the land as it is in every other technologically advanced nation. **Healthcare is not a privilege, but a basic human right.** Health insurance companies must go the way of the dinosaur and take their rightful place in the trash bin of history, as there is no single capitalist practice more barbaric than medicine-for-money and denying people healthcare for lack of funds.

"As civil rights leader, **Dr. Martin Luther King, Jr. (1929-1968)** noted, *'Of all the forms of inequality, injustice in healthcare is the most shocking and inhumane.'*

"Unfortunately, my brother, Ben, was a victim of the medicine-for-money Ponzi scheme we call the American healthcare system," said Antonelli. "You see, Ben suffered from schizophrenia and mental illness is, perhaps, the least addressed health issue in our society—which makes sense if you consider it through a capitalist lens, since **mentally ill people are not productive, can't hold down jobs and consequently, don't provide profits for the ruling class.**

"Ben wandered off to points unknown, and was homeless for quite some time. We had no idea where he might have gone. For years, every time I passed a homeless person on the street I'd check to see if it was Ben. It was terrible! However, Ben's homeless wanderings did not help him to escape from his mental demons, who apparently continued to haunt him until one day he went into a far-too-accessible gun shop in Florida, bought a pistol and committed suicide. I'll never forget the day that I got the phone call from the Tampa police. No words can express my shock, pain and anger at a society that treats its most vulnerable citizens with such utter disregard and, indeed, contempt. I miss Ben every day. He is a major motivator for me to get out of bed in the morning and continue my life-long work on behalf of justice. Justice for Ben and all the other casualties of predatory capitalism is what keeps me engaged in The Struggle."

Antonelli, wiping a tear from his cheek, then posted another powerpoint slide, saying, "Here's a partial list of nations that provide some form of universal, taxpayer/government supported healthcare to their citizens. You'll notice that some are wealthy, first world, technologically advanced countries and others, not so much.

Nations With Universal Healthcare

Australia, Austria, Bahrain, Belgium, Botswana, Burkina Faso, Brunei, Canada, Cyprus, Denmark, Finland, France, Germany, Greece, Iceland, Ireland, Israel, Italy, Japan, Kuwait, Luxembourg, Netherlands, New Zealand, Norway, Portugal, Singapore, Slovenia, South Korea, Spain, Sweden, Switzerland, United Arab Emirates, and the United Kingdom.

(Source: Wikipedia https://en.wikipedia.org/wiki/List_of_countries_with_universal_healthcare#Burkina_Faso)

"If they can do it, so can the wealthiest nation on the face of the earth," Antonelli concluded. "All that's lacking is the political will."

Chapter 24

The Way Forward

"We now see many long oppressed groups of working class people organizing and demanding justice," Antonelli said. "The rise of numerous, seemingly disparate organizations, each demanding justice for a particular oppressed group bodes well, especially if they are conscious enough to see that they share a common oppressor; predatory capitalism and then, come together and demand justice with one powerful voice. Groups like Occupy, Black Lives Matter, #metoo, Never Again, The Dreamers and Labor Unions all confront the same opposition; predatory capitalism. They must resist the temptation to fight amongst themselves and stride together toward a more just economic, social and political tomorrow. **If activists can avoid petty bickering amongst themselves and, instead, embrace the intersectionality of their common cause in solidarity, practicing radical empathy, much will be accomplished.**

"Democratic Socialism has proven itself to be the most effective form of social organization for securing essential and fundamental needs and protections for the average citizen. Norway, a democratic socialist country, ranks first in the United Nations survey of nations with the highest quality of life for the average citizen." https://www.cbsnews.com/news/un-norway-has-best-quality-of-life/

"We could learn much from the experiences of the people of Norway which can be applied to our societal problems," continued Antonelli. "If we follow their lead we too can create a government good enough for everyone; that addresses human needs not private greed. Focusing on worker's issues is the tide that lifts all boats and addresses the concerns of all seemingly disparate social justice organizations. We all want and need healthcare, housing, education, a living wage and a dignified retirement regardless of race, color, gender or sexual orientation. This approach will encourage unity amongst the diverse social justice organizations and help prevent the ruling class from splintering our movement with divisive wedge issues and purity litmus tests. **We, as the working class, the 98 percent, must learn to treat each other with radical empathy, understanding that we have all been victimized by predatory capitalism and only radical empathy for each other's unique experience will galvanize our solidarity.**"

The Two Party Conundrum:

"So, can all of this be accomplished within the parameters of a calcified two party political system, driven by money and special interests? THAT is the question!" exclaimed Antonelli.

"In the post-capitalist age, our political institutions must reflect this dynamic new social consciousness and either evolve or be replaced by new organizations which better reflect the beliefs and values of democratic socialism; namely, democracy and radical empathy."

"Today's Republican Party is essentially co-opted entirely by wealthy, ruling class interests; is intellectually bankrupt and morally malnourished. It has little to offer us except the tired old repeatedly failed trope of Supply Side/Trickle-Down Economic Policies—what I earlier referred to as a 'Chew and Screw.' This leaves us with only the Democratic Party as a potential option within the present political landscape. Unfortunately, much of the Democratic Party has also been purchased by the same ruling class oppressors and all too often, doesn't represent a dramatic difference in social policy. However, the Democratic Party does represent the best possible host for co-optation within the establishment," noted Antonelli.

"Let's not, however, fall prey to false equivalencies," Antonelli warned, "the two political parties are not equally destructive. The Democrats provided virtually every social safety net program ever enacted by the federal government; from Social Security to Medicare, Medicaid, minimum wage and unemployment insurance, Civil Rights and voting rights legislation, as well as protecting women, children and the LGBTQ community. Not to mention the Affordable Care Act (aka Obamacare) and the DACA program.

"Meanwhile," he continued, "history informs us that all of these programs have been vehemently opposed by the Republican Party, which ceaselessly attempts to cut or repeal many of them to this very day. So let's not fall prey to this kind of 'pox upon both your houses' mentality which only serves to muddy the waters and provide political cover for much of the unconscionable conduct of Republicans. After all it was a Republican who denied a Democratic president his constitutional right and responsibility to nominate and attain a vote on his nominee for the Supreme Court. Then Senate Leader, Republican Mitch McConnell did precisely that for nearly one full year until Republican President Donald Trump won a questionable and controversial election and appointed a conservative justice to the 'stolen seat.' All working people, women and minorities seeking justice will pay dearly for that stolen seat for decades to come. The Supreme Court of the United States has become something akin to nine politicians in robes and the Republican appointees have, for the most part, never seen a corporation they didn't love.

"The question and challenge for most progressives and democratic socialists of every stripe is this," said Antonelli, "do we set out on our own and create a new third party or instead, attempt to co-opt the Democratic Party? **Do we essentially reinvent the wheel or take back the steering wheel from the Democratic Party and redirect it, returning it to its traditional role as the party of working people?** History has not been kind to third party initiatives and in the age of Citizens United, the political parties often serve as little more than cash registers, so it's not an easy question to resolve. Perhaps the way forward is to do both simultaneously. We can both, work to enlist and promote truly progressive and democratic socialist candidates within the Democratic Party and also use those same grassroots methods to build a growing consensus for a third party approach should one be needed in the future. All of which would serve to educate the public about the benefits of democratic socialism and help transform public conscience as it did with recycling and Earth Day. The looming threat of Democratic Socialists breaking off and forming a third party will, if nothing else, serve to get the attention of corporate Democratic establishment leaders.

"What we want to avoid, indeed <u>must</u> avoid," he warned, "is creating divisive litmus tests that only serve to weaken the people's movement and further empower the predatory capitalist class. **Divisiveness amongst Socialists/The Left only serves to benefit the Ruling Class.** Unfortunately, no one does circular firing squads like democratic socialists and The Left. They undermine their own interests when they condemn would-be allies for not being 'socialist enough' or thinking differently about some particular issue, or not fully endorsing their particular version of change. Unfortunately, in a two-party system you will often likely be confronted with a lesser-of-two-evils ballot. Remember this: **When you don't vote for the lesser of two evils, the worst evil often wins.**

"I played football in high school," recalled Antonelli, "and they always coached us to fall forward when being tackled. While it may not be a lot, falling forward always adds a little yardage to your effort. Democratic Socialists need to learn how to fall forward when supporting candidates who don't entirely agree with their views but have enough in common to advance some of the progressive agenda. Let's not make the perfect the enemy of the good. It's quite unlikely that you will ever encounter another person who agrees <u>entirely</u> with your views so don't shun someone who agrees <u>mostly</u> with you. We aren't electing saints and no one is perfect- including ourselves so hey, maybe we could be wrong about some particular pet issue? We need to support candidates who advance <u>most</u> of our views since we will be hard pressed to find anyone with whom we agree 100% of the time. **Unity need not require uniformity**. Let's strive to be pragmatic Social Democrats, realizing that the achievable will always fall short of the ideal, but nevertheless, persisting. That's the political version of **'Falling Forward'**. Take the yardage that you can get on the play and continue to advance the ball."

Chapter 25

Late Stage Capitalism and the Gig Economy

"We are presently living through a particularly barbaric period known as late stage capitalism." Antonelli said. "The good news is that predatory capitalism is nearing its end as a destructive, exploitative economic system. The bad news is that this is the exact point at which capitalists, having fully exploited people and planet and who can no longer expand profits globally, begin consuming the very social institutions and infrastructures that had previously sustained them. They now strive to decimate essential social programs like Social Security, Medicare, Medicaid and public schools in order to give themselves still greater tax breaks. Privatizing schools, infrastructure projects and even military services, and instigating wars all in the name of profits.

"Automation presents the capitalist class with further motivation to destroy programs essential to working people since labor is increasingly less useful to their production needs. Indeed, bare bones, skeleton crews already staff many factories and production facilities. There's perhaps no more brutal example of this mechanized cruelty than the enormous factory farms where utterly unspeakable atrocities are regularly committed against our fellow living, sentient creatures such as chickens, pigs and cows while still other machines systematically inject poisonous chemicals into our crops and the earth itself. In any event, we are now living through the stage when capitalists literally cannibalize their own cultures, much like a snake devouring its own tail, recklessly destroying the very planet itself, extracting every last penny of profit." Antonelli said.

"This phase, Capitalism's death throes, of course presents the greatest threat to working people as what little semblance of social safety net is cut away from under them and they struggle to survive in the new **'Gig Economy'** where low paying, benefit-free, part-time jobs make up an ever greater sector of the economic landscape. One cannot survive, much less thrive, in an economy built on employment in the fast food industry or ride share and food delivery companies. The average age of today's fast food worker is 29, according to the Bureau of Labor Statistics. This is no longer an 'entry level' job traditionally held by high school and college kids. It's now a form of subsistence.

"On the bright side, however, the increasing realization of this new economic reality should motivate many more workers to take social action on behalf of a more sustainable future." Antonelli said. "This will occur as worker alienation and dissociation reach epidemic levels and the working class rises up and demands change and justice. Indeed, the ever growing numbers of the Precariat will soon have nothing to lose.

"When a critical mass has concluded that the present economic system is no longer sustainable, change will occur just as it did with the advent of Earth Day and the expansion of environmental consciousness. But these shifts do not occur of themselves, they must be advanced by real people demanding real change in real time.

"Dr. King said that, *'The arc of the moral universe is long, but it bends towards justice.'*

"However, it's very important to remember that the arc doesn't bend of its own volition," stressed Antonelli. "**The arc of the moral universe must be bent toward justice by socially conscious, justice-loving people of good will who stand up and demand change.** Democratic Socialism is not something to be feared but rather embraced as it has demonstrated its ability to uplift the quality of life for diverse cultures across the planet. Indeed, it's the continued barbarity of the existing capitalist system which makes life into a kind of dog-eat-dog, survival of the fittest ordeal. This we do, indeed have many good reasons to fear. We should all celebrate predatory capitalism's rapid demise on the human landscape; casting it aside as a barbaric chapter in our collective evolution as a species."

"But isn't capitalism the way we've always done things?" asked Tony.

"We used to accept slavery too," replied Antonelli. "As well as women's inequality. Gay people were relegated to the closet and minorities once 'knew their place' as second class citizens in American society. We now understand that all of these once conventional wisdoms were nothing more than established ways of oppressing others. It was the way we had always done things. We now celebrate our strides away from these foolish and oppressive behaviors.

"As **Ralph Waldo Emerson (1803-1882)** said, *'A foolish consistency is the hobgoblin of little minds...'*

"And that, Reeya," said Antonelli turning towards her, "is precisely why politics and social activism is so critically important. It's the only means by which we can collectively remove foolish consistencies and destructive practices and create a humane, sustainable and just society. Now do you see the significance and critical need for political activism? It's far too important to be left to the politicians," said a smiling Antonelli.

"And as the ancient Greek philosopher **Plato (c. 427-347 BC)** said, *'The price of apathy towards public affairs is to be ruled by evil men.'*

"**The truth is that Democratic Socialism is as American as apple pie, FDR, LBJ, and the Constitution.** Indeed, the Preamble, the very first sentence of our Constitution, clearly states that taking care of our people is a primary purpose of our government," Antonelli said, while reaching into his coat for a well-worn pocket edition of the constitution, which he always carried with him. "'We the people of the United States,'" Antonelli read aloud, "'in order to form a more perfect union, establish justice, insure domestic tranquility, provide for the common defense, ***promote the general welfare***, and secure the blessings of liberty to ourselves and our posterity, do ordain and establish this Constitution of the United States of America.'

"History demonstrates that there is simply no better way to 'promote the general welfare' than Democratic Socialism," concluded Antonelli.

Chapter 26

Reeya's Revelation

Just then, the bell rang, ending classes and students gathered their things to leave. Reeya, deeply moved by all that Antonelli had to say, remained behind to further discuss what she had learned this day.

"I'm starting to see what you're saying, Mr. Antonelli," she said, placing her books and presentation posters down on Ms. K's desk. "I'm beginning to understand that I do, indeed, have a part to play in creating a more just and sustainable society and planet. I can also see how democratic socialism is the most direct and effective path toward that humane, sustainable global tomorrow. It's radical empathy in practice.

"This idea of social activism," she continued, "is truly in accord with the teachings of the Bhagavad Gita, a sacred text of my Hindu faith, which also encourages taking ACTION in the material world."

"That's right, Reeya," Antonelli replied. "**Ideas only transform the world when they change our collective behavior and that requires action.** Deeds, not words."

"Democratic Socialism should not be feared but embraced," he continued. "It's a system which only further empowers people and doesn't restrict but expands democracy and freedom in both government and the workplace. It's only common sense that people should have a say in events that directly impact their lives. **There are very few problems within a democracy that can't be better addressed by more democracy.** And in a wealthy and moral nation, no one should live in poverty, without access to healthcare, education and housing. It's not about 'free stuff,' as some critics charge, since everyone provides funding through equitable taxation and consensus based budget prioritization—driven by human need, not greed. And it's not entirely about taking over the means of production but rather seeing that everyone shares equitably in the fruits of their labor and has an equal voice within the means of production and receives their fair share. It's actually what's sometimes called a **'Mixed Economy,'** which provides governmental control of the essentials for equality such as healthcare, housing, education and the like, while regulating equity and fairness within the private sector by requiring living wages, a voice for labor in the boardroom, maternity and paternity leave and the like. **Political and Civil Rights are essentially meaningless if not accompanied by Economic Rights.** For example, what does it matter if a black man has the right to eat at the same lunch counter as a white man if he can't afford to buy a sandwich? **True Justice requires Social, Political and Economic Justice**," said Antonelli

"So, in order to truly honor the values of Earth Day," said Reeya, "I must do my part and actively work for justice on behalf of all inhabitants of this planet as well as the planet itself. And not only practice toleration but fully embrace the idea of 'unity through diversity' which Earth Day founder John McConnell so often stressed.

"But how can I both make my way in a brutal capitalist environment, find a job and make a life, while working to change the system?" asked Reeya.

"Ah, there's the rub!" said Antonelli. "**You must ride the bicycle while fixing it.** By that I mean attend to your career, pursue your life goals but never forget where you came from and always assist and empower other working class people in their struggle. You won't have to look very far to find oppressed working class people. Just consider the people here today, for example; Jamal's African-American heritage, Fiorella's citizenship issues, Ms. Kaufman's sexual orientation and my ethnic, working class challenges. **While each struggle is unique, we are all victims of the same oppressive capitalist system.**

"There's no shortage of work to be done, Reeya," he said, smiling. "We must honor and respect the experience and suffering of all working class people regardless of their historically and socially constructed position in the capitalist hierarchy. The vast majority, the 98%, are indeed <u>all</u> oppressed by the capitalist 2%. The era of being a footnote to history is over for women, Blacks, Latinx, LGBTQ, and all working people, provided we have each other's back and see each other through the lens of **Radical Empathy**. The sheer numbers, the demographics are on our side.

"Join groups of people with similar consciousness and conscience, who share your goal of social, economic, political and planetary justice," continued Antonelli. "Work relentlessly in support of the oppressed everywhere. And strive to be that person who, through their actions, reflects the values of justice in your day- to- day life by practicing **radical empathy**. World renowned physicist and democratic socialist, **Albert Einstein (1869-1955)** said that we *'must widen our circles of compassion and embrace all living things and the whole of nature in its beauty.'*

"A big part of the purpose of family, historically, has been an attempt to make a safe place in an unsafe world. **We must ex-**

pand and widen our definition of family to include <u>all</u> of Earth's inhabitants as well as the planet, itself," said Antonelli.

"Oh, yes! Now I think I understand something that my dear, departed Dadu, Grandpa Deepak often told us," Reeya recalled. "He was a great admirer of the Indian independence movement leader ***Mohandas K. Gandhi (1869-1948)*** and would often urge us to ***"Be the change we seek in the world."***

"That's definitely how I understand **Radical Empathy**." Antonelli said. "Caring about the well-being of all of Earth's inhabitants and the earth itself. Taking the love which we normally reserve for family and extending it to our entire earthly family. When we cut the chains of fear, all that's left is love. And that love, that Radical Empathy, makes it impossible to accept the cruelty of predatory capitalism oppressing any of our brothers, sisters and the planet. Always ask yourself **'How can I be of service?'** and you aren't likely to go too far amiss," Antonelli said, pensively.

"As one of my favorite rock stars from my heydays**, *Jimi Hendrix (1942-1970)* put it, *'When the power of love overcomes the love of power the world will know peace.'***"

"Wow!" exclaimed Reeya, "I'm starting to understand how important this work actually is! But how much difference can any one person really make? The problems seem so overwhelming!" she sighed in exasperation.

Antonelli considered Reeya's question for a moment, then responded, "Yes, Reeya. Sometimes, the immensity of our problems can, indeed seem overwhelming. Those are the moments when it's good to remember the story of the old man and the beached fish. Once there was an old man walking along the seashore where he encountered thousands of fish that had been beached by the previous night's storm. They laid flipping and flopping helplessly awaiting death on the damp sand. The old man, seeing their plight, began to slowly and methodically pick up the fish, one by one, and toss them back into the sea–back to life. Just then, a young man came along and seeing the seeming futility of the old man's rescue efforts in the face of an entire beach covered with fish, shouted, 'Hey, foolish old man, what difference can your efforts make in the face of so many fish that need your help?!' To which the old man thoughtfully held up a fish and replied, 'It makes a difference to this one,' as he tossed it back into the life- saving waters.'" Antonelli said. **"We start where we are. We do what we can; as much as we can. That's Radical Empathy in action.**

"We were once a people who did great things," Antonelli recalled. "We won World War Two, built an interstate highway system and went to the moon. We did so, as **President John F. Kennedy (1917-1963)** said, *'not because it was easy but because it was hard.'* We need to become those people again. If we are to solve the problems we face we must have the courage to think in new, creative ways. As Democratic Socialist**, Albert Einstein** (1879-1955) said, *'We cannot solve our problems with the same level of consciousness that created them.'*

"Some things are worth fighting for," continued Antonelli, "even if you lose. While theory provides an essential foundation, it's action that relieves the suffering of everyday working class people. Deeds, not words. Let radical empathy be your moral compass. It will guide you to doing the right thing. Trust in your compassion, your heart. Always ask 'How can I be of service?' This will assist and guide you during the inevitable rough patches. And never, ever let anyone or anything tarnish your integrity. Your integrity is all that you take with you to the grave. Be sure that your legacy is an honorable one, worthy of emulation not condemnation."

"You must nevertheless, persist," he said. Just then it occurred to Antonelli to reach into his weathered tweed jacket pocket and pull out a silver wrist band.

He handed it to Reeya and she read its engraved message aloud: **'Nevertheless, She persisted'**.

Antonelli continued, "I was given this wrist band by the parents of a former student named Cathy Landry. She was very much inspired by what she learned in my class and became active in social justice issues. Apparently, she was constantly feeling ill but her family couldn't afford to see a doctor so they hoped it would pass. Finally, when she could no longer stand the pain, her family took her to see a physician who diagnosed her condition as cancer. It had progressed significantly while her parents were unable to afford her medical exam. Indeed, it might even have been caught and cured had she seen a doctor sooner. She died within a few short months of her diagnoses and her parents wanted me to have her bracelet. I've been carrying it around ever since as a reminder of the importance of our work. I want you to have it. Wear it proudly and let it serve to motivate and inspire you during the difficult patches on the road to social justice."

"You want me to have this?!" Reeya exclaimed. "Oh my! It's beautiful! And such a wonderful inspiration! Thank you so much!"

Antonelli replied, "No need to thank me...you can best thank Cathy and all the other 'Cathys' out there by persisting in your efforts for justice."

"Thank you so much!" said Reeya while gently caressing the shiny silver bracelet now resting upon her wrist.

Then Reeya, considering Antonelli's words, casually picked up the kaleidoscope from Ms. Kaufman's desk. Putting it to her eye and slowly turning it, Reeya was captivated by the panoply of shapes and colors. She suddenly realized that this was a wonderful representation of the earth and all its inhabitants; together forming a miraculous whole by uniting the very distinctly different peoples and cultures to create a beautiful, diverse and colorful planetary landscape.

"Yes!! Yes!" she exclaimed. "Now I see what Earth Day founder John McConnell meant by 'Unity through Diversity!' And that I do, indeed, have a critical role to play in the planet's future. It's now my generation's turn to take up the torch of justice and do our part to advance it, just like those medieval cathedral builders who knew they would never see the end result of their work but had the faith to do their part in order to create a better, more beautiful future world.

"It's now my generation's turn to advance the cause of economic, social, political and environmental justice," she said, "We must strive to leave our children and our children's children with a more humane, sustainable world than we inherited from our parents...sometimes, one fish at a time.

"Practicing Radical Empathy," Reeya said, determinedly, while gazing at her new bracelet, affirming aloud, "and 'nevertheless, persisting'."

And so The Struggle continues.

THE END....of the beginning.

"We live in Capitalism, its power seems in-escapable—but then so did the divine right of kings. Any human power can be resisted and changed by human beings."

Ursula K. LeGuin, American Writer (1929-2018)

(Ursula K. Le Guin (2016). "Words Are My Matter: Writings About Life and Books, 2000-2016, with a Journal of a Writers Week", p.115, Small Beer Press)

#ResistWithReeya

A Few Books to Hang Out With

Books are listed by topic, in no particular order. Check out the books/websites that interest you, the others may get your attention some other time. Trust your instincts and follow your bliss. I've attempted to provide the least expensive editions where possible. Books listed may be available for lower cost in downloadable formats and used condition. Note to those who may say this list is incomplete: You're right.

American History/Earth Day:

People's History of the United States by Howard Zinn (2015) New York. Harper Perennial Modern Classics, Reissue Edition.

Lies My Teacher Told Me: Everything Your American History Textbook Got Wrong by James W. Loewen (2018 Reprint Edition) New York The New Press

A Disability History of the United States by Kim E. Nielsen (2013) Boston. Beacon Press

A Young People's History of The United States: Columbus to the War on Terror by Howard Zinn, adapted by Rebecca Stefoff (2009) New York. Seven Stories Press.

Earth Day Network Website:
https://www.earthday.org/earthday/

Earth Day: Visions of Peace, Justice and Earth Care: My Life and Thought at Age 96 by John McConnell, John C. Munday (Editor), Aye Aye Thant (Foreword) (2011) Resource Publications

African-American Studies:

So You Want to Talk About Race by Ljeoma Oluo (2018) New York. Seal Press Hachette Book Group.

When They Call You a Terrorist; A Black Lives Matter Memoir by Patrisse Khan-Cullers and asha bandele (2018) New York St. Martin's Press.

Letter from Birmingham Jail by Dr. Martin Luther King, Jr. Note: This open letter is available on-line at: https://www.africa.upenn.edu/Articles_Gen/Letter_Birmingham.html

Strength to Love by Dr. Martin Luther King, Jr. (2010) Minneapolis, MN. Fortress Press

Stride Toward Freedom: The Montgomery Story by Dr. Martin Luther King, Jr. (2010) Boston. Beacon Press

Why We Can't Wait by Dr. Martin Luther King Jr. (2000) New York Signet Classics

A Testament of Hope: The Essential Writings and Speeches by Martin Luther King Jr.,

James S. Washington (Editor) (2003) New York. HarperCollins Paperback.

Autobiography of Malcolm X as told to Alex Haley (1987) New York. Ballantine Books

Malcolm X Speaks: Selected Speeches and Statements by Malcolm X (1989) New York. Pathfinder Press

100 African-Americans Who Shaped American History by Chrisanne Beckner (1995) San Mateo, CA. Bluewood Books

Democratic Socialism:

Bernie Sanders Guide to Political Revolution by Bernie Sanders (2017) New York. Henry Holt (BYR) sold by Macmillen Publishers

Where We Go From Here: Two Years in the Resistance by Bernie Sanders (2018) New York Thomas Dunne Books an imprint of St. Martin's Press

What is Socialism and Why is it Important in America? Exploring Socialism from Karl Marx to Bernie Sanders by Ryan Rogers (2018). Independently Published. Kindle available.

Why Socialism? By Albert Einstein Note: Article available on-line at:
https://archive.org/details/AlbertEinsteinWhySocialism

Dreamers/DACA/Latinx Studies:

How Does It Feel to Be Unwanted? Stories of Resistance and Resilience from Mexicans Living in the United States by Eileen Truax. Translated by Diane Stockwell (2018) Boston; Beacon Press

Dreamers: An Immigrant Generation's Fight for Their American Dream by Eileen Truax (2015) Boston Beacon Press

100 Hispanic-Americans Who Shaped American History by Rick Laezman (2001) San Mateo, CA. Bluewood Books

Education:

Pedagogy of the Oppressed: 50th Anniversary Edition by Paolo Freire (2018) New York Bloomsbury Academic, Bloomsbury Publishing, Inc.

Democracy and Education by John Dewey (2015) Createspace Independent Publishing (reprint of 1916 original publication)

The Schools Our Children Deserve. Moving Beyond Traditional Classrooms and "Tougher Standards" by Alfie Kohn (2000) First Houghton Mifflin Paperback New York

Reign of Error: The Hoax of the Privatization Movement and the Danger to America's Public Schools by Diane Ravitch (2014) Vintage Reprint Edition New York

Badass Teachers Association website:
http://www.badassteacher.org/

Indigenous People/Native American Studies:

An Indigenous People's History of the United States by Roxanne Dunbar-Ortiz (2014) Boston Beacon Press

Bury My Heart at Wounded Knee by Dee Brown (1972) New York Bantam Books

Black Elk Speaks: Being the Life Story of a Holy Man of the Oglala Sioux as told to John G. Neihardt (1972) New York. Pocket Books- a Division of Simon & Schuster

The Primal Mind: Vision and Reality in Indian America by Jamake Highwater (1981) New York Meridian the Penguin Group.

LGBTQ:

A Queer History of the United States by Michael Bronski (2012) Boston. Beacon Press

The Gay Revolution by Lillian Faderman (2016) New York. Simon & Schuster; Reprint Edition

Transgender History; The Roots of Today's Revolution (second edition) by Susan Stryker (2017) New York. Seal Press, Hachette Book Group.

<u>Women's Studies/"Herstory":</u>

The #MeToo Movement (21ˢᵗ Century Turning Points) by Laurie Collier Hillstrom (2018) Santa Barbara, CA. ABC-CLIO Publishing

Everything Changed; The Amazing Journey of American Women from 1960 to the Present by Gail Collins.

America's Women; Four Hundred Years of Dolls, Drudges, Helpmates and Heroines by Gail Collins

Through Women's Eyes: An American History with Documents by Ellen Carol Dubois and Lynn Dumenil

100 Women Who Shaped World History by Gail Rolka (1994) San Mateo, CA. Bluewood Books

Acknowledgements

"It takes a village to raise a child" declares an African proverb. And so it seemingly takes a city to write a book. I am fortunate, indeed, to have more people to thank than I can mention here and I will attempt to keep this list brief. However, I first and foremost, wish to express my deepest love and gratitude to my wife of nearly thirty years for providing not only constant support and encouragement but the most precious of gifts to any writer; time to write this book. Tanti Baci!

I'd also like to thank my closest friends who span decades, for their encouragement during the critical moments of the writing process. So, at the risk of inadvertently overlooking someone, a big shout out to the chemist and street poet known as "stevenj", whose weekly phone conversations are usually worth getting up early for on Saturdays.

To my dear friend Nik B. and his late wife, Sumitra who literally fed my body and mind back in our grad school days, and Michael Mario D. who fed my soul in those "bad old days". And to Robyn T., who's known me for so long that we once attended a concert featuring a new opening act from California called the Eagles. The band seemed promising. Wonder whatever became of them?

To Brett Peruzzi of Peruzzi Communications for developing an initial marketing plan, identifying and developing outreach opportunities which assist with telling people about my book.

To Colby Groves. Without his creative technical savvy, social media acumen and publishing industry experience, *Reeya's Earth Day* might well still be sitting in dry-dock.

And thanks to my dearly departed parents, Dan Sr. and Genevieve and brother, Gus who, alas, didn't live to see any of this. Hope I'm making you proud.

And to my teachers, Bill K. and Elliott E. who provided guidance and support to a first generation college kid from the ethnic working class and encouraged him to think and dream big.

For my students, who always inspire and motivate me and urged me to tell this story.

To the beloved memory of my two deceased shelter cats, Key West Charlie and Chuckie, who taught me so much about the power of love and radical empathy in the face of great adversity.

And, finally, special thanks to the people and dynamic energy of the city of Austin; the creative nexus of Texas.

Dhanyavaad Bahut, Grazie Infinite, Muchas Gracias, Thank You!

About the Author

Dan Camilli grew up in a Boston working class family. The first in his family to graduate high school, Dan went on to earn graduate degrees from both Harvard University and the University of Maryland at College Park after earning a B.A., Magna Cum Laude, from the University of Massachusetts at Boston (Formerly Boston State College).

An award-winning educator, curriculum writer, and a Massachusetts Teacher of the Year nominee, Dan received a Fulbright Distinguished Awards in Teaching Scholarship to China, Hong Kong and Taiwan. He then continued his studies in Japan as a Keizai Koho Fellow. Dan was then awarded a grant from the National Endowment for the Humanities to conduct independent research to further develop curriculum for his innovative and popular history, philosophy and world cultures courses.

Dan created and hosted a podcast called "Nature, Sport and the Spirit" where he interviewed award-winning playwrights, sculptors, painters and others about their passion for what they do and their experience with the creative process. He is a columnist and blogger, writing about topics as diverse as the nature of time; impact of technology on our ability to communicate and the cultural importance of honoring teachers.

A self-described working class kid with a ruling class education, Dan never forgot where he came from, and his courses have inspired multiple generations of high school and college students who continue to work for social, economic, and environmental justice. These days, Dan hangs his hat in Austin, Texas. The site of his childhood home is now a Valvoline Instant Oil Change location.

Reeya's Earth Day is Dan's second book. The first, entitled *Tee Ceremony; A Cosmic Duffer's* ™ *Companion to the Ancient Game of Golf* has been described as "a delightfully lighthearted and humorous introduction to philosophy cleverly disguised as a book about golf." "Views golf as a walking meditation—a kind of yoga with clubs."

Visit **dancamilli.com** for columns, blogs, podcasts, and more.

NOTES

NOTES

NOTES

Made in the USA
Middletown, DE
21 April 2019